I0626621

SNOWED BY THE WALLFLOWER

Revenge of the Wallflowers

CAROLINE WARFIELD

Merlin's Owl Press

ISBN: 978-1-7332450-6-7

Cover art by Mandy Koehler

met him during all that business in Lords that so occupies you gentlemen."

He murmured that he had not.

The bold chit took his arm. "Do come and meet Maman. She would so like to meet you," she said giving his arm a tug.

BELINDA SURVEYED the artfully arranged dishes on their porcelain platters and judged them adequate. She would remind Carlton to clean the silver tomorrow after she sent off her order for supplies. She'd managed to cobble together a decent sauce with what was in the larder. Spices were there aplenty from Belinda's last visit. Mrs. Wesley, the cook, never touched them. The estate supplied plenty of beef, mutton, and fish, and its succession houses could be counted on for greens and fruit.

Taking a quick glance in the bottom of a shiny pot, she tidied her hair, and judged herself adequate as well. Aunt Violet expected her at dinner, but Belinda couldn't be certain whether she would be missed or not. She shook out her skirts and headed toward the drawing room.

The room's main doors were closed. The stationed footman would open for her, but Belinda preferred not to make an ostentatious entry. She knew a smaller door opened on a servant's pantry. No one paid attention to it. She slipped through the pantry and into the drawing room without notice. The company buzzed with first night anticipation. Gentlemen young and old huddled near Uncle Hartwell's decanters; matrons in full feather gossiped in ones and threes; and the eager young women clustered together as if there was safety in numbers. Belinda stood quietly behind a chair in which Viscountess Bellachat held court. Nearing eighty, the woman held herself past the age where manners mattered. She amused Belinda—most of the time.

"Look at them. Throwing themselves at him as if he were a prize stallion and they the farmer's least favored mares," the old lady grumbled.

"He's the biggest prize this year, Mabel," another matron replied. "Duke's heir. This bunch hopes to get the jump on the fillies coming up next Season."

She means the much-vaunted earl, of course. She wondered how the earl would feel being compared to a breeding horse. It would serve him right. Being ogled as if she were a brood mare on auction had soured Belinda on the whole Marriage Mart business. Then again, it might puff up his male ego.

She glanced at the men at the end of the room, recognizing only a few of the older gentlemen. Which might be the earl? One rotund man going thin on top looked a likely candidate. So did the chinless fellow next to him. No eager misses clustered around either of them, however. There was no sight of Cecil either.

Two ladies moved, and she caught sight of Sophie smiling up at a tall gentleman while her friends stood, wide-eyed, nearby. If that was the earl, he was far from the faded roué Belinda expected. When he tipped his head to listen to Sophie, candlelight reflected off the thick honey-gold waves of his hair. Sophie obviously found him enthralling, and, peering at his broad shoulders and strong back, Belinda could see why a naïve young thing might be infatuated. She tamped down her own unbidden and unwanted jolt of attraction, swallowing the sudden lump in her throat.

Dinah Beckwith sailed over to Sophie's circle. The Season's diamond two years ago, she had turned down two younger sons, a viscount, and baronet. Belinda thought her a harpy who would settle for no less than a duke or a marquess—or the heir to one. Poor Sophie.

Doors to the dining room opened on the far right. "Dinner is served." Carlton's announcement woke Belinda from her absorption in Sophie's companion just as he turned and she saw his face.

That is no earl! Belinda's stomach curdled. John Conlyn, author of Belinda's greatest humiliation, the fiasco at the Duchess of Haverford's charity Venetian outing, stood across the room, as gloriously handsome and untrustworthy as ever. He had been absent the previous season, along with Cecil's circle of reprobates; she'd hoped he was gone for good.

That man can't be the earl. Can he?

While Belinda watched, Aunt Violet took Conlyn's arm, "As highest-ranking guest…" she trilled, gazing up and him and parading toward the dining room. Belinda's lunch threatened to make a reappearance.

The higher-ranking guests formed partners and moved toward the dining salon in proper rank, and the rest prepared to follow, but Belinda couldn't bear the thought of food. Even worse, she couldn't bear being at the same table as the wretch whose prank had all but ruined her.

She moved as quietly as she could to the left side and slipped back into the servant's pantry, almost jostling a tray of glasses in the arms of a footman. "Sorry, George," she whispered. The irritated footman continued out into the hallway and toward the kitchen. Assuming no guests would be in the hall, Belinda popped out behind him.

Too late, she realized the hall wasn't empty.

"Oh dear, Harry, it's my cousin the Wescott Menace," Cecil sneered as he approached with one of his toadies.

Both looked deep into their cups, and they hadn't even been to dinner yet. "I wondered when she would get here!"

"Isn't she the one so bad she made everyone at Haverford's lawn party retch up their luncheon? We best be on guard." The toadie giggled.

"True enough. Can't even serve a proper tea. How is the Nuisance Collective, Cuz? Still disgusting every man in the ton with their bold behavior and crackpot ideas?" Cecil sneered.

Belinda's face burned at the hated nicknames. Cecil toddled on and she didn't dare challenge his words.

In the end, she couldn't resist tossing words at his back. "You best move quickly, Cec. You wouldn't want to risk your dear mummy's wrath by being late for dinner!"

It was a lame attempt. Cecil ignored her jab. He kept repeating "Nuisance Collective" and laughing at his own wit. "Thank goodness the mater didn't invite them all," he proclaimed as the two worms slithered into the drawing room and off to dinner at the end of the guests just in time.

He referred, of course to the Nemesis Collective, a pact Belinda and friends made to stick together for mutual defense after enduring their first three terrible seasons. Belinda dearly wished they were here, except both Ariadne and Merrilyn had married during that awful season in which so many people at the Duchess's Venetian breakfast became violently ill after eating food Belinda made. The fashionable world blamed her for their distress, shunning her much of the waning weeks of the Season. Sophie's mother, Aunt Flora, hadn't allowed her near the London kitchen since then.

It had not been her fault. One sight of Cecil and his friends laughing told her all she needed to know about who slipped emetics into her batter. They had pranced through

Aunt Flora's kitchen, teasing and harassing her. She knew they must have done it while they distracted her.

She'd been dubbed the Westcott Menace ever since. She always believed the haughtiest churl in their group came up with that witticism, the only one who had sufficient brains. John Conlyn.

Chapter 3

BEFORE JOHN COULD RESPOND to the woman who'd clamped on to his arm, they were called to dinner, and couples formed in the correct order. The Earl of Hartwell led the ranking female guest in, and John found himself called upon to escort the countess who paraded head high into the dining room.

He gazed about, but the interesting woman he'd noticed before had disappeared to his disappointment. He helped countess to her seat and resigned himself to his fate. He could only hope dinner was an improvement over the night before.

At least he wasn't seated near Dinah Beckwith. He had seen her from afar surrounded by suitors at the few events he attended two years before. Younger, in her first Season, she dominated the scene even then. He would have to watch himself around that one.

The countess seated him to her right with her niece on his other side. He began to turn his head toward Lady Sophie when another person, straggling in at the end of the group, caught his attention. Lord Cecil Hartwell. John

I dedicate this story to all young women who have yet to find their own power and brilliance

had been informed the wretch would be hunting in the north and not in attendance, or he wouldn't have come. He'd been informed wrongly. *Damn.*

Lady Sophie leaned over conspiratorially. "I don't like him much either. And he's my cousin," she said under her breath.

He barely suppressed a bark of laughter at that. Lady Sophie had backbone. And good taste. John had become involved with the miscreant when he was at his lowest. He regretted every wasted moment.

The butler waved a hand and the soup course began. John still saw no sign of the woman who had so fascinated him, neither as a servant nor as a guest. *Odd that.*

He dipped his spoon in the soup, still studying the guests across from him. What he tasted sent his eyebrows upward. It was an excellent white soup, well-seasoned with a hint of leek and a correct sprinkle of ground almonds. He took another spoonful.

Very good indeed. "My complements on the soup, Lady Hartwell," he said.

The countess straightened with a smug smile. "My cook is excellent."

She must have been missing last night if that is so, he thought.

The dinner progressed easily—each successive course delicious, the conversation requiring little effort.

Lady Sophie proved able to converse on topics other than the weather and the latest fashions. She had at least a basic knowledge of politics and had read more than novels. Lady Hartwell seemed quite content to let him focus his attention on her niece, sparing him her fawning.

Between a decent course of fricasseed rabbit and a platter of rather fine glazed lamb cutlets with haricot beans, Lady Sophie leaned toward Lady Hartwell. "Where is Bel, Aunt?" she asked.

"Bel?" he echoed.

"Belinda Westcott, my other niece. *Miss* Belinda Westcott," Lady Hartwell said through tight lips. "She was meant to join us, but she must have become indisposed." She glared at Lady Sophie, the expression passing so quickly he almost missed it. "Perhaps you'll meet her later," she said.

Belinda Westcott. The name tickled his memory. Perhaps she was the woman he had noticed earlier. But no—that woman was hardly indisposed.

The moment passed. He enjoyed the lamb and the variety of pickles served after. He turned his attention to the countess. "My complements to the cook, Lady Hartwell. What wonder can we expect for the fruit course?"

The countess appeared briefly disconcerted. "I—" She wiped her mouth. "That is, I can't recall. There is so much to plan for an event like this, you know."

"You have obviously gone to great lengths for your guests, Ma'am. I thank you."

The countess's cheeks grew pink, her pleasure obvious. After a sweet dish of spiced pears and clotted cream, she rose to her feet to lead the ladies out. She smiled to her husband at the far end of the table, and with steel in her voice not quite masked by a girlish laugh she said, "Don't linger overlong, my lord."

Lady Sophie and the others followed her out, leaving John dreading he might be forced to converse with Cecil and Lord Harry Smithers, his groveling follower. He had no interest whatsoever in renewing those particular acquaintances.

Unfortunately, when the gentlemen moved toward the end of the table, John's position put him squarely in front of Cecil

John leaned toward the head of the table as Lord Hartwell led the conversation toward the price of corn and the old king's health. He still had much to learn, and was willing to listen, although he already knew he'd hear little to assist in the problem of unemployed soldiers or the impact of prices on tenants. His grandfather had been much more open on those topics.

Meanwhile, Cecil gulped down his port and held his glass for another, nudging Harry who leaned back, bored. The two miscreants brought back bad memories of his own behavior.

John needn't have worried. Having decided he'd stayed long enough, Cecil lurched to his feet saluting his father with his second glass before downing it. "Off to the billiard room!" He ignored the Earl of Hartwell's frown and pulled Harry up by his arm.

"Coming with us, Ridgemont?" Cecil slurred.

"No, thank you. I will stay and enjoy the conversation."

Cecil shrugged and toddled off, but, as he passed, John heard him sneer, "You didn't used to be such a dull stick, Ridgemont."

Chapter 4

"BEL! WHERE HAVE YOU BEEN?"

Bel cringed when Sophie's voice caught her half way up the stairs. She had lingered too long in the kitchen and now she couldn't make her escape. She turned, hoping Sophie thought she was on her way down not up, forced an apologetic smile onto her face, and stepped down the rest of the way while ladies flowed into the drawing room behind her cousin.

"I took a nap after speaking with Cook and overslept," she lied as smoothly as she could. Perhaps not smoothly enough if Sophie's quizzical expression was any gauge. "I thought to join you for tea. Was Aunt Violet cross?"

Sophie's cheeks went pink. "I'm not sure she cared."

Of course, she didn't!

Sophie hooked her arm on Bel's elbow. "You're here now. Come to tea with the ladies." She leaned in and whispered, "Wait until you meet the earl! Such a delightful gentleman."

Bel's stomach did a flip. *John Conlyn is no gentleman*

The bevy of ladies fluttered about the drawing room,

settling themselves as Bel and her cousin came in behind them. Aunt Violet, busy directing some of the younger ladies, didn't notice.

Tea service arrived, brought by George and one of the younger footmen. "Will Miss Bel serve, my lady?" George asked glancing at Bel.

Aunt Violet peered around the room, spied Belinda retreating behind Viscountess Bellachat, and tittered, "If you would, my dear. The group is so large, your young bones are better able to manage the thing."

Bel rose and murmured, "If you wish, aunt."

"Ladies, this is my elder niece, Miss Belinda Westcott." A puzzled look came over Aunt Violet's normally placid face. "She was, er, indisposed earlier."

A few quiet acknowledgements followed. One or two of the matrons frowned, no doubt recalling The Westcott Menace. Bel felt as though every eye in the room drilled into her back but she approached the tea cart and began to direct the footmen with a flourish. The young men placed plates of sweets on strategically located tables.

Soon, Bel followed the tea cart around the room, ascertaining each lady's preference for lemon, sugar, milk, or none of them, and gracefully gesturing to the sweets. She began with the most senior ladies clustered around Aunt Violet.

"Still unwed, I see, Miss Westcott," Viscountess Bellachat pronounced reaching for a lemon cake.

"Perceptive as always," Bel replied with a smile, moving on.

The viscountess's bosom bow, Lady Arncastle, frowned at Bel and glanced at the tea she was handed; she sipped cautiously. None of them would dare make a scene or refuse to take tea from Bel in front of the formidable

Countess of Hartwell, Aunt Violet, but they all remembered the Haverford incident.

Bel thought about the dinner they had just eaten, most of it prepared by her own hands, and continued with an amused smile, indulging every one of them, even Dinah Beckwith, who posed, artfully arranged, on a settee that had been placed strategically across from the door through which the men would enter in due time. She took a cup but ignored Bel as if she were a servant.

"You are cheerful," Sophie murmured when Bel reached the youngest ladies.

"Of course," Bel said. "I live to serve."

"Bel, honestly!" Sophie remonstrated. "Don't speak so of yourself. Come and sit by me, and I'll introduce my friends."

It soon became clear that the two or three young ladies nearest to Sophie were indeed friends, or on their way to becoming so. Bel was glad for her. They chatted about the house party, their plans for winter, and their families, encouraging and complementing one another. They traded reading suggestions. If a few of the young people sitting a bit farther away appeared bored, Bel found that predictable. Across the way Dinah, chin raised, glanced over disdainfully.

Sophie would meet many less kind people, some outright hostile, among the Ton. Friends had been Bel's only defense among them. She had formed the Nemesis Collective with Merrilyn Parkham-Smythe and Ariadne Hollingsworth as a defense against the sharp claws of other ladies and the predatory advances of the men. Now both Ariadne and Merrilyn were married—and both deliriously happy. Bel dreaded going on alone. Sophie's little group warmed her heart for her cousin's sake.

A hint of movement and indrawn breath was Bel's only

warning before the door opened and the men trooped in. The earl and an older gentleman led the way. Two of Cecil's dandyish friends followed, and two very young gentlemen. Bel ignored all of them. Against her will, her gaze riveted on one man—the Earl of Ridgemont, John Conlyn—and an involuntary shiver of attraction shot through her at the sight of his broad shoulders, great height and hair so thick she wanted to run her fingers through it.

He needs a trim, she thought absently, before snapping her jaw shut and sitting straighter. *Don't be a ninny, Bel.* She dragged her eyes back to her cousin, but not before she saw Dinah Beckwith rise and skillfully block Ridgemont's progress into the room before he could choose a seat.

He didn't look unhappy, Bel thought irritably. *They are well matched. Nasty pair.*

She concentrated on her cousin's friends, shutting out Aunt Violet. Shutting out the biddies watching her. Shutting out Conlyn.

"They are staring," whispered Lady Ella Manning, who sat next to Sophie. Bel followed the direction of her gaze, as did their entire little circle, to the young men slouched near Uncle Hartwell's decanters. Jaded and cynical to a man, Cecil's crowd, most of them. They probably made sport in mocking the girls.

"Have you met the Honorable Peter Hartley?" she asked, diverting the girls' attention to a young man sipping tea with Lady Bellachat and clearly amusing the old woman. "He is, I believe, the son of the Earl of Westhampton."

One of the ladies sitting on the outer edge of their circle leaned toward Bel. "Isn't he a cousin of the Marquis of Aldridge?" she said, quivering with excitement.

"I believe so," Bel said, "But he is nothing like him."

Aldridge was well known as a rake, as dissolute as they came. Still, Bel had never known him to be cruel. Perhaps Peter Hartley resembled him in that much at least. She sighed. Young women could be dangerously foolish.

Bel rose and leaned forward to agree with a surprisingly clever comment about the writings of Walter Scott. She intended to move on to greet other ladies, but she felt warmth at her back just before a deep male voice vibrated through her. *John Conlyn. Ridgemont.* "Well said, Lady Joanna, and charmingly put."

A bright pink blush gave Lady Joanna Mitchell an appealing glow. Sensing his closeness, Bel feared the heat on her own cheeks would be a mottled red. She did not turn. Perhaps he would ignore her.

"I'm afraid I haven't met your companion as yet, Lady Sophie." His voice sounded like the low rumble of thunder in the distance. She had noticed it two seasons ago when he asked her to waltz, a dance interrupted by a laughing Cecil. That was when she had first realized he was not the gentleman he appeared, but one of the low-lives who flocked with her cousin.

"Of course, my lord," Sophie chirped. "Bel, may I present the Earl of Ridgemont?" Bel turned slowly to face the wretch. "My lord, may I present my cousin, Miss Belinda Westcott?"

Bel froze. She gazed up into deceptively innocent appearing hazel eyes, and held her breath when they narrowed. He blinked, and she saw the flicker of recognition.

"I'm honored," he said with a polite inclination of his head, all the while studying her face with care. Dinah Beckwith, she noted, still clung to his arm. Was it Bel's imagination or did the girl's fingers tighten at his words?

Would it matter if I ran from the room? Of course, it would.

Bel swallowed. Hard. "The honor is mine," she said curtseying properly before turning to peer at Miss Beckwith in an attempt to avoid his penetrating inspection, only to face a viper's hateful glare.

"How are you enjoying my aunt's hospitality, Miss Beckwith?" Bel crooned with faux concern. "You appeared weary sitting there moments ago."

"Well enough," the girl responded. "At least dinner was decent tonight."

"I respectfully disagree. It was beyond 'decent.' I would rate tonight's dinner excellent and look forward to seeing what other treasures the cook creates this week," Ridgemont said. "I asked Lady Hartwell to pass on my regard to the cook. The glazed lamb was particularly fine."

Sophie's friends murmured their agreement, mentioning favorite dishes. Flattering though the praise was, Bel began to make her excuses and move on. Unfortunately, the Beckwith creature spoke first.

"Did you find the dinner satisfying as well, Miss Westcott?" She gave "Westcott" an almost imperceptible twist, but Bel caught the hint at her hated nickname, and the reference to her great humiliation.

Bel forced a cold smile to her lips. "Certainly, Miss Beckwith. Our cook is a genius in the kitchen." *And I should know since I am she.* "Now, if you will excuse me, I promised Lady Arncastle a tour of the gallery, and we've yet to arrange it." It was a lie, but also the first excuse that came to mind.

WESTCOTT. *The Westcott Menace.* The way Miss Beckwith said the word brought it back. John groaned inside. He had been such an ass that year. He watched Belinda Westcott walk away, head high, and knew she'd caught the jab as well.

John hadn't been at the Haverford Venetian breakfast in which everyone who had sampled savories from a particular platter—the one rumored to have been the offering of Belinda Westcott—had fallen ill.

He heard the story of the Haverford disaster—in painful detail—from a chortling Cecil Hartwell late that same night when they were deep in their cups. His involvement with Hartwell shamed him.

John had been invalided home from Spain to recover from a persistent fever, and couldn't shake humiliation at being laid low. It had been years since he spent time in London, and he'd been a veritable greenhorn when he'd fallen in with a group of disreputable scum—Lord Cecil Hartwell and his cronies— while he waited for orders and transport back.

The night of the Haverford fiasco, Cecil, the reprobate, took great delight in describing which of society's darlings had lost their luncheon in the rose bushes or, worse, on the lawn. The horrid nickname emerged from that late night drinking binge. *The Westcott Menace*. He didn't recall who came up with it, but he rather feared the bacon-brained wit had been himself, may the saints preserve him from an excess of drink ever again.

Only later had it slowly dawned on him that Cecil and company had likely contaminated his cousin's dish with an emetic, thinking it a great joke. The prank had been too successful for the miscreant not to take credit. John removed himself from their company after that—or tried to. Then his grandfather had called him home, demanding he leave the army.

A tug on his arm brought him back to awareness. He had been staring at Miss Westcott. Dinah Beckwith clung to his arm like a barnacle. He could think of no delicate way to extract himself, reluctant to add poor manners of his own to her obvious unladylike behavior.

"I do so love house parties," Miss Beckwith crooned. "Winter can be so lowering. I am certain Lady Hartwell will have plenty of things planned to keep us warm and… cozy. Don't you agree?" Her eyes promised more coziness than a young lady ought.

Lady Sophie and her circle of friends peered up quizzically. "Lady Hartwell, my aunt, does enjoy planning these gatherings. Her parties are known for activities designed to keep all her guests mingling with one another," Lady Sophie said. She gazed directly at John, amusement in the slight quirk to her lips.

John smiled back at Lady Sophie. "I'm glad to hear it. There are many people here I'd like to know better." He extracted his arm from Miss Beckwith's grasp with a firm movement. "In fact, I see some gentlemen I wish to greet, if you would excuse me ladies."

Before he could move, Lady Hartwell called the room to attention. "I'm sure you must all be weary from travel," she began. Belinda Westcott, he saw, helped Lady Bellachat to her feet.

"We are that, Violet," Lady Bellachat declared tartly. Nervous laughter greeted her words.

"There will be entertainments most evenings, but for tonight, I think it best we make an early night of it," the countess went on. She glanced around the room with mischief in her expression. "You'll need energy for tomorrow. I've received confirmation that our pond is frozen solid and ready. We'll begin tomorrow with a skating party! Hartwell Hall keeps a store of skates of all sizes ready for guests. There will be fires for warmth and warm drinks as well."

"Some of us are too old for that nonsense, Violet!" Lady Bellachat objected loudly.

"Of course. Cards, books, and an array of snacks will be available for those who don't wish to enjoy the opportunity," Lady Hartwell said. John saw Miss Westcott frown, though why that bothered her he couldn't say—unless she would be expected to arrange the activities for the elderly.

Lady Sophie had risen to her feet. "Do you skate, Lord Ridgemont?"

"It has been a long time, but yes. I'll look forward to some vigorous activity," he replied.

The Beckwith chit gripped his arm again. "It sounds ever so delightful, but I fear I don't know how to skate on ice. Do say you will help me! I'll need a strong arm," she said fluttering her eyes.

John felt trapped. "I will certainly look forward to escorting young ladies on the ice."

Something suspiciously like a choking sound came from Lady Sophie's throat, quickly swallowed. "I thought you longed for—what was it? Warmth or cozy time by the fire?" she asked.

Miss Beckwith tossed the words away with an impatient hand. "There will be plenty of time for that. Later." She said through tight lips.

"I wonder what else my aunt has planned," Sophie mused with faux innocence. "If it snows, there could be sledding. Certainly, a brisk walk—the dales border the earl's land. I hope you brought sturdy boots."

John managed to avoid laughing out loud. "It sounds strenuous. I'd best get my rest," he said, pulling his arm away.

"I will see you tomorrow," Miss Beckwith said, her voice throaty with promise. "Perhaps you can help me put on my skates."

There was no polite way to refuse. "Of course," he said.

"Perhaps we can take a turn around the ice, Lady Sophie," he said.

Lady Sophie beamed up at him. "If you can find time for me, that would be lovely," she said, glancing mischievously at a glowering Dinah Beckwith.

"I'm sure I'll manage." John caught sight of Belinda Westcott moving toward the door and hastened his departure. "Ladies," he said with a nod and hurried away.

He reached his quarry in the hallway. "Will you skate tomorrow, Miss Westcott?" She tipped her head and slowed.

"I fear not. I have some tasks that will require my attention," she said.

Her aunt's dogsbody—no doubt about it. "Pity," he replied. "Perhaps we shall see each other in the evening."

"Perhaps. Good night, my lord." She left him standing there.

John reached the suite he'd been assigned with relief and began unwinding the everlastingly tight cravat. Graves, who had been waiting, brushed his hands away and assisted him.

"Graves, do you remember me speaking of Miss Belinda Westcott?" he asked.

"Not as I recall, my lord." Graves began unbuttoning his waistcoat while John's mind roamed back through the evening, passing quickly over the giggling girls and viperish Dinah Beckwith to settle on the woman who so fascinated him when he saw her directing servants in the dining room. Belinda Westcott.

"Wee bit distracted tonight, are ye? I asked if you're wanting yer banyan," Graves prodded.

John nodded, still puzzling over Miss Westcott. What

was it about the woman? The confidence he first noticed. The warmth of her voice, chatting and laughing with her cousin. Her perfect dignity. The gentle way she dealt with the quarrelsome old woman. The sway of her hips, the line of her back, and her determined stride when she walked away.

He sat in the wing-backed chair by the hearth and thanked Graves for the glass of brandy he offered. A smile lifted John's face and warmed his heart. At least one woman had attracted his attention tonight. He determined to get to know her better, but the pride in her bearing when she gave him short shrift before saying good night suggested it would not be easy.

"Very well, Miss Westcott," he murmured into his drink. "I do enjoy a challenge.

Chapter 5

BEL RETURNED TO THE KITCHEN, after brushing past Conlyn—Ridgemont—but didn't get far in her preparations for the following day's meals and Aunt Violet's mandated snacks before she was invaded.

Cecil and two of his friends wandered in loudly demanding to see what there was to eat. Cook wrung her hands and the two little kitchen maids hovered in the corner, wide-eyed.

"Cecil! You needn't disrupt the kitchen. Ring for a foot man if you require service," Bel declared wiping flour from her hands.

Cecil pranced around the table. "When the Westcott Menace has her hands in, we have to inspect our vittles carefully," he scoffed setting off a round of laughter. "Came down to inspect." He grabbed the jar containing yesterday's biscuits, reached in, and began tossing them to his friends. "Wesley, did you or the Menace make these?" he demanded.

Mrs. Wesley glanced frantically between Bel and her employer's son. "I done 'em, my lord," she whispered.

"Stop terrorizing the kitchen, Cec. Take the biscuits and go," Bel demanded.

He tossed a few more, ignoring the ones that hit the stone floor and shattered, stuffed several in his pockets, and sneered at Bel. "Menace!" He shouted, striding toward the door where he spun around to face her again. "The Westcott Menace—Ridgemont came up with that one. Did you know that, Bel? Next Season's big fish calls you a menace. Wait until we drop *that* in the ear of the gossips," he laughed. He pelted his friends with another biscuit and left, leaving silence in his wake.

Bel wanted to follow and throttle him. Instead, she had to rally her staff. A half-hour later, breakfast had been prepped, dinner planned, and she was well on her way to a third batch of cakes and biscuits.

"Thank you all, but get you off to bed. Breakfast will come early," Bel told them. She lifted the chin of the most capable of the kitchen maids. "Remember, Annie. I trust you to support Mrs. Wesley. And also—do be careful in salting the eggs. I plan to sleep late after I finish up the baking tonight."

Much later—Bel suspected midnight had passed—she sat, alone and weary, at the worn and marred wooden table to enjoy an herbal tisane before finding her own bed. She leaned her elbow on the table, her head on her hand, no longer able to keep thoughts of Cecil's horrid behavior at bay.

Cecil had made her life a misery since he cut off one of her braids when she was six. Their grandfather, informed by the gardener, had called Cecil on the carpet and given him a birching. Cecil blamed Bel. When Grandpapa died a few years later, Cecil blamed Bel that he was excluded from the will as well. His behavior toward her worsened.

Aunt Violet's blindness to it all was a familiar ache. There would be no point in complaining about him. His threat to ruin yet another Season, however, left her desolate. If only she could convince Aunt Flora to give up trying to present her and allow her to withdraw to the country. If only they would release her dowry into her own keeping.

She took a sip of her tisane and shook with a sigh. Cecil had confirmed one thing. John Conlyn—his preening lordship of Ridgemont—had created her hated nickname and would be at the center of more humiliation in the Spring.

She sat up straight in her chair when an idea came to her. *There is no use trying to live it down; I could just as well use it.*

If Ridgemont and Cecil wanted to paint her as a menace, she should treat them to a dose of her talent for chemistry. She could humiliate them before they did it to her, and get her revenge at the same time. Her reputation would be same in the end.

Bel pushed herself up with both hands. She lit a candle, unlocked the room she had converted to her laboratory, and searched bottles until she found it, a vial of *Cephaelis ipecacuanha* that she had distilled into a syrup. The perfect emetic.

She stared at the bottle while finishing her tisane. She could make sure it went up to Cecil and his friends with their breakfast tea or coffee, but they would be so ill from drink they might not even realize it. No, she needed something public. If she wanted to make someone vomit, she needed it to be outside to avoid damage to Aunt Violet's parlors.

The skating party would be perfect.

She considered methods to get something laced with *ipecacuanha* to Ridgemont alone, and avoid other guests. If

Bel planned carefully, she could slip him tainted hot chocolate. She could count on George to help. Dinah Beckwith planned to force Ridgemont to partner her. Beckwith might get some also, but Bel wouldn't weep over that.

Let the skaters beware! Bel blew out the sconces and carried her candle up to bed.

THE NEXT MORNING, John waited at the front door bundled in a warm coat and scarf, hat in hand. He hoped to catch sight of Belinda Westcott, though she insisted she would not skate. If he were lucky, he might escort Lady Sophie Gilray to the lake.

A sound on the stairs caught his attention, and he saw Lady Sophie on the first-floor landing. He started to smile, but Dinah Beckwith shouldered past her and danced down the stairs to ambush him.

"Are the coaches ready?" she asked, clamping on to his arm, and forcing John, who had planned to walk, to follow her.

After much fussing and demanding that she be wrapped warmly under coach blankets and pouting when a footman carried out the wrapping rather than John, they finally set out with Miss Beckwith squeezed next to Lady Sophie and another lady with John on the back-facing bench next to Walter Davis, a cheerful gentleman who seemed to be a friend of Peter and who quite looked forward to skating. John wished he had stayed in bed.

The pale sun glistened off the lake when they arrived, however, and his mood lifted. Footmen arranged skates on a table set up for that purpose and tended fires placed in barrels around the nearer banks of the lake. John helped the ladies from the coach and escorted them to benches set near the fires.

Miss Beckwith tossed him a coy look. "Please find me a small pair of skates," she demanded "I have very tiny feet." He couldn't politely refuse.

When he found lady Sophie examining the skates carefully and selecting a pair, he rather admired her independence. "May I request that we take at least one turn around the lake?" he asked.

"Perhaps after Miss Beckwith tires out, "she responded, gazing at him sympathetically, amusement bright in her eyes.

John sighed. "I'll count on it," he said.

It didn't take long. He had no sooner escorted Miss Beckwith out and gone a few feet, before she slipped artfully to the ice. "Oh! my ankle, "she moaned. "Please take me back to the bench"

The bench, of course, was inadequate for her terrible agony, or so she said. "I simply can't do this. I'll have to go back to the house. Please take me back to the house." She batted her eyes at him.

John turned away and looked around. The coach had returned with more guests. "You there," he called to one of the footmen. "Run and stop the coach from returning. Miss Beckwith has injured herself and needs to go back to the house." She beamed up at him with a triumphant gleam in her eye.

Triumph faded once John asked one of the stronger footmen to carry her to the coach, and he bid her farewell. "Oh no, I—" The footman looked at John who nodded, and the boy kept going to deposit her in the coach.

She glowered back, saw him watching, attempted a pathetic expression, and fell back against the seat.

"Not heroic of you, my lord." Sophie stood at his side.

She peered up with a hint of mischief. "But very effective," she said.

Neither of them voiced what they were thinking. Dinah Beckwith was no more hurt than Sophie. "May I help you with your skates Lady Sophie?"

She lifted a foot already fixed with a skate. "I'm quite capable of doing it myself. I've been skating on Uncle Hartwell's lake since I could walk."

They did two turns on the lake before she called to her friends. Peter Hartley and Walter Davis joined them and soon the young people were laughing and chasing one another.

A half-hour later, John did a circle around Lady Sophie and came to a stop in front of her, quite admiring the color in her cheeks and the fun in her expression.

"It appears sustenance has arrived," he said, nodding at the footmen carrying baskets to the table on the shore. "Shall we see what is on offer?"

They skated to the edge, where ginger cakes and various biscuits could be had. Tall crockery jugs with spouts were wrapped in towels to keep tea and chocolate hot. Sophie peered over the choices.

Before John could ask her if she wanted tea or chocolate, George the footman reached under the table and pulled out a thick flagon with a stopper. "We have a stronger chocolate for gentlemen," he said. He poured out a mug and handed it to John.

Laced with spirits, no doubt.

Sophie shook her head in irritation. "They always treat ladies as if we were fragile!"

It wasn't an unfair complaint. When he offered her the mug, her head bobbed up, and she searched his face. Seeing approval, she took the mug and took a quick sip. Her brows drew together, and she stared into the drink.

She took another sip. "Sweet. Different. Good, I think," she said and proceeded to down the chocolate.

John saw George give her a wide-eyed stare. *Who is a footman to approve or disapprove?*

Sophie raised her shoulders sheepishly. "I must have been made hungry by all this exercise," she said. She reached for a ginger cake.

"One for you, my lord?" George handed another mug from the flagon toward John.

John considered for a moment. If there were spirits in Sophie's mug, he'd best keep a clear head. "I believe I'll have tea," he said.

George frowned and dumped the chocolate on the ground before he fetched a clean mug, pouring tea for John.

Others crowded around the table, and John led Sophie aside. He didn't offer her a second mug, and she didn't ask. They nibbled ginger cake in silence while he drank his tea. "Something warm hit the spot," he said.

"I agree. It was a treat. Shall we take a loop of the lake while the ice is relatively empty?" Sophie asked, rising to her feet and stepping on the ice. She glided away, taking a graceful spin and moving out. He followed her, relieved to see that she appeared to be fine.

Within minutes, everything changed.

One moment she was skating in circles, laughing. The next her face paled and her joy disappeared. "I think I've overdone it," she whispered, slowing, and raising the back of her hand to her forehead. He reached her as she came to a full stop.

"I feel dizzy. Too much spinning," she whispered.

John suspected she had imbibed unaccustomed spirits too quickly. He put his arm around her and turned her toward the shore. "Forgive me for being forward, Lady Sophie, but I think you need to sit for a while."

She nodded. A moment later she moaned, "I feel horrible."

They were almost to the shore when her ginger cake made an abrupt return, and chocolate followed it to the ground. "Sweet mercy," she groaned. John pulled out his handkerchief and handed it to her, navigating to the bench all the while.

He encouraged her to sit and lean over, her head on her knees. She vomited again, losing her breakfast and more. She murmured "I'm sorry so sorry," over and over incoherently.

This is too much for a drink of spirits. Something is terribly wrong.

John removed her skates and his own. One of the younger footmen ran over and took them, while John lifted her into his arms. "When will the coach be back?"

"Not soon, I fear. There's a pony wagon, my lord. We used it to transport the food," the boy said. "It isn't much…

By then her friends had circled round, some of the ladies terrified, the gentlemen offering assistance.

"I'll take her up to the house. You and the others make sure the footmen pack up all the food and drink. Don't touch any of it! Something is very wrong."

Peter took charge, directing the nearest footman to show John to the cart, and ordering the others to stop serving food and drink.

Minutes later Sophie lay on her side in the back of the little wagon, towels cradling her head while John drove as fast as he could to the kitchen yard of the manor house. When he lifted her, she demanded to get down, and promptly got sick into the herb garden.

He gathered her up, burst into the kitchen, and barked orders like the lieutenant colonel he once was. "Summon Lady Sophie's maid and the countess. She has become ill. I'm taking her to her room." The sight of Belinda Westcott startled him. What was she doing in the kitchen? She had flattened herself against the wall and gone pale, as if she saw a ghost.

"Miss Westcott, your cousin needs assistance. Kindly show me to her room." He marched through the green baize door to the public rooms without waiting for a reply.

Chapter 6

BRUSHING PAST RIDGEMONT, Bel knelt by the bed, pulled off Sophie's pelisse, and began unbuttoning her gown. "Susan, fetch Lady Sophie's nightgown! Also, water and clean toweling," she said without looking up. The girl scurried away.

Bel sensed the earl hovering behind her, but refused to look at him. "You must leave, your lordship. Spare my cousin her blushes." She turned to fetch a cloth from the washstand and came face to face with him, still in the doorway, his expression grim. He wasn't peering at Sophie; he was studying Bel.

"I asked you to leave. A gentleman would…"

He blinked. "Yes, of course. I will go back to check on the rest of the party. I had the food locked away, but who knows how many people were sickened."

Bel's stomach clenched. *How did George bungle my orders?*

"We will talk about this when your cousin is well, Miss Westcott. We *will* talk about this." He left before she could answer him.

Angels above, did he guess? Bel forced the thought away. She had to focus on what she'd done to her cousin. There would be time for guilt and remorse later.

Susan returned with fresh water. "Let me help with that gown, Miss Westcott." The two of them had her out of it soon enough, and washed the worst of the sick away.

At Bel's orders, the maid fetched lavender soap, and they washed her again before removing her soiled chemise. In all the commotion, Sophie groaned and begged for a basin. Long minutes later, the girl lay back limp and pale, her eyes closed. They managed to get her into a clean nightgown without setting her off again.

"Fetch the clean wash bowl from the washstand in my room and then empty this one," Bel ordered.

Bel laid wet cloths on Susan's forehead. The incoherent noises Sophie made worried her. The dose in the flagon had been prepared for a man of Ridgemont's size and weight. It was far too much for a little wren like Sophie.

She grabbed up a paper from the tiny desk in the corner of Sophie's room and wrote out instructions for fetching peppermint and yarrow. She didn't trust the kitchen to make the tea so she asked for the containers.

Susan returned, set down the clean basin and picked up the dirty one. "Can you read, Susan?" Bel asked.

"Not well, miss. But I know my letters," the girl replied.

"Good. Look at these words carefully." Bel pointed to the names of the herbs printed on the bottom. "Ask Mrs. Wesley to let you in my laboratory and fetch the jars with these names on them. Only these two. Can you do that?"

"I think so, Miss. Will it help my lady?"

"Yes. It should. Tell Mrs. Wesley we need hot water, a large teapot, and a footman to help you fetch and carry. Do you understand?"

"Yes, miss." Susan dashed off.

Bel sank to the chair, and picked up Sophie's hand, wallowing in guilt and fear. Perhaps Sophie had expelled the *cephaelis ipecacuanha syrup* completely—all Bel could do was hope, soothe her, and try an herbal tisane to calm her stomach.

Aunt Violet burst through the door. She leaned over to Bel's ear and whispered. "I heard… That is, did Sophie become ill on the ice? Carlton told me Ridgemont marched right through the house and up the stairs carrying her."

While Bel took a moment to formulate an answer, Aunt Violet went on breathlessly. "Ridgemont! Think of it. And several people saw. There is talk downstairs, and Dinah Beckwith is quite out of sorts over it."

"Ridgemont was a perfect gentleman. Her stomach was—"

"Yes, yes!" Aunt Violet waved unpleasant words away. She dropped her voice again. "Talk may reach London. Whatever will her mother say to me."

"There is no scandal, here, Aunt," Bel said. "At least not to Sophie."

Aunt Violet gasped. "Has anyone else been sick? This isn't another one of those… Those accidents, is it?" She didn't have to explain what she meant by "another."

"There was nothing deliberate," Bel said through clenched teeth. That was not entirely true; Bel intended the tainted hot chocolate. But Sophie hadn't been the target. "I don't believe anyone else has taken ill. Ridgemont has gone back to make certain."

"Then Sophie got some spoiled food. This time I will truly fire the cook. Even you can't keep her tip top." She rose and shook out her skirts. "We'll just have to contain the scandal."

Susan interrupted them, followed by two footmen carrying two teapots, fresh sheets, and fresh towels. Susan bobbed a curtsey to the countess, glanced from one woman to the other, and handed Bel two vials. "I hope I did this right, Miss."

Bel examined the containers of herbs. Peppermint and yarrow. "Exactly right, Susan. Thank you.

"Sophie will get well, won't she?" Aunt Violet asked belatedly, a slight squeak in her voice.

"I believe so, though she may be weak for a day or two. We'll do our best to ease her upset," Bel replied.

"Good. I will manage the talk. Still, Ridgemont's care is all to the good, I expect." With a swish of skirts, she left Bel to attend her cousin, clean up the sick room, and try not to worry about the loss of the compliant Mrs. Wesley in the kitchen.

NO ONE else had become ill. Not one other person. The young people had continued their fun as if nothing had happened, but they all skated over when John arrived to ask about Lady Sophie. He assured them she would be well.

With relieved smiles and happy waves, they skated on. John hoped he was right about Sophie's condition. He was certain now that the chocolate in the "gentlemen's" flagon had been the source. He was equally certain it had been intended for him, not his partner. He couldn't forgive himself if she was injured in his place.

When he looked for the flagon, however, it had disappeared. So had the footman, George, who had been eager to dump out the remains after Sophie took the mug.

Why would a footman try to humiliate a guest? He wouldn't.

John pondered that issue as he marched back to the house, certain the footman may have been an accomplice, but he wasn't the perpetrator.

By the time he reached the front steps, he was equally certain that, however much Belinda Westcott may have been an innocent victim in the episode at the Haverford venetian breakfast, she was guilty as sin this time.

But why?

John stood in front of Lady Sophie's suite and feared he knew why. Guilt curled up his neck. He turned to leave. After all, he had no business in a lady's room. Several steps later he stopped.

Miss Westcott didn't intend her actions for her cousin, much less anyone else among the guests. She must be worried sick.

She answered his knock promptly. "Come in, George."

"It isn't George," he said, a spurt of anger pushing other emotions aside. "How is she?" he asked from the doorway.

Miss Westcott glanced over her shoulder and back at the girl on the bed. "Better. We seem to have quieted her stomach, but she is weak." The lady rested quietly, to John's relief.

"If you have more instructions for your collaborator they will have to wait."

Miss Westcott leapt to her feet and turned to face him; eyes wide. "I— I don't…" she choked out.

"We'll worry about George when we have that conversation that I promised you. I came to tell you no one else got sick. You didn't hurt anyone else."

The relief in her expression was palpable. Pride quickly brushed it aside; she raised her chin. "What do you mean? Are you assuming the *Westcott Menace* is at work here?"

He cringed when she threw the horrid nickname in his face. She had backbone; he'd give her that.

"There is no assumption. I'm sure of several things. We'll speak about them when Lady Sophie is well." He turned on his heels and gave her no opportunity to answer.

Chapter 7

LADY SOPHIE and her elusive cousin remained above stairs the following day and night. John burned to intrude, though to see which of them, he couldn't say. By afternoon, a choice between whist with the elderly or a snowy hike through the home wood faced him. Once again, he found himself in the middle between the aged and the energetic crowd a few years younger than he in age yet many more years younger in life experience. He chose the walk.

Peter Hartley met him at the door, warmly garbed and wrapped in scarves. "Do you have any news about Lady Sophie?" His interest seemed more than casual. In the unlikely event that John decided to pursue the girl, he would have competition

"She was well by late afternoon yesterday. I haven't heard anything new. She was weak, however, and in need of rest."

Others joined them in a cloud of chatter and energy. As they turned to leave one more joined the party.

"I'm just in time." A miraculously healed Miss Dinah

Beckwith clamped on to his arm possessively. For the next three quarters of an hour, she managed to keep the others, particularly the young ladies, at a distance by use of cutting comments and the frowns he saw reflected in the others' eyes when she thought he wasn't looking. She babbled on about "poor fragile Lady Sophie Gilray."

As they made the turn to go back, he'd had quite enough of his persistent pest and extracted his arm, drawing a petulant pout.

"Pity not to put all this snow to use," he declared, drawing all eyes, some confused, some wary. He struck Peter with a well-aimed snowball, and the melee was on.

The group arrived back at the manor wet, rumpled, and laughing. Miss Beckwith, who had gone rigid with indignation the only time a snowball came her way, had stalked off much ahead of the group. He watched her safely to the manor from a distance while the snowballing moved in that direction. Lady Ella Manning and Walter Davis, Peter's deceptively shy friend, had been declared winners.

John bowed over Lady Ella's hand. "I applaud your prowess with a snowball. I will see you at dinner." The young lady's cheeks, already ruddy from the cold turned a darker shade of red. He snapped an ostentatious military salute to Davis and took the stairs two at a time.

His suite, which he strongly suspected was the finest guest suite, lay on the second floor. As he reached the first, the urge to pound on Lady Sophie's door seized him, but the state of his coat and boots stopped him.

The firm *tsk* with which Graves greeted him affirmed he was wise to postpone seeing the ladies.

"Has there been any news about Lady Sophie?" John asked, handing over his greatcoat and sitting so that the clucking valet could remove his boots.

"These'll be ruined you keep this up," Graves muttered.

"Lady Sophie?" John prodded.

"Word in the servants' hall is she's taking tea and toast. They reckon she'll be right as rain by tomorrow."

"That's a relief. What about Miss Westcott?" John asked.

"Stayed with her cousin all night. Maids think she's a saint. Caused a fuss in the kitchen, though."

"How's that?"

Graves wandered into the wardrobe, returning with a heavy banyan and towels. "Get you dry and warm," he said.

"About the kitchen, Graves!"

"The countess swanned in and accused the cook of poisoning the niece. Said she'd let her off without a reference. The Westcott woman got wind of it and swooped down to announce it wouldn't happen. Said the countess would forget it in a week and told Mrs. Wesley—she's the cook—to just lay low. Cheeky that. It ain't her household."

"I suspect she knows her aunt." *I suspect she feels guilty.*

Dinner that night was dismal, almost as bad as the first night. John puzzled over the wide swing in quality while neglecting both Lady Hartwell on his left and Lady Emma Manning on his right. Every time he looked up, Dinah Beckwith's scowl curdled his stomach. Perhaps that or Cecil Hartwell's presence assaulted his taste buds, not the actual quality of the cooking.

Cecil cast a sly glance toward his mother and leaned across the table to whisper with a hiss, "Afraid of the food, Ridgemont? Is a menace on the loose?"

The countess shot her son a lethal glare of disapproval, and the miscreant sat back.

John poked at the overcooked mutton on his plate. *Is a*

menace on the loose? Not in general; the attack had been precisely targeted. More to the point, the cook from two nights ago was obviously out of commission. The conclusion was clear. John knew exactly where he could corner Belinda Westcott.

"QUIT FUSSING, Bel. I am quite well!" Susan had Sophie in a comfortable yet attractive day dress the following morning and had done her hair in a simple knot at the back. Sophie did indeed appear well.

Bel drew in a deep breath. "Very well. Just remember you are still weak. Try to sit and let others take care of you."

Sophie refused an arm with an eyeroll. "I will do just fine. You get yourself to the kitchen and see if you can unravel the mystery. What made me ill?" She marched off, leading Bel to follow and Susan to clean up the sick room.

Ladies were gathering as they reached the breakfast room; they encountered Lady Bellachat at the door. The old woman raised her lorgnette and peered at Sophie owlishly. "None the worse for your ordeal," she sniffed. "Bit pale. Perhaps you can explain what had Ridgemont parading through the house like a madman looking for your quarters. Not the done thing. Seeking a woman's room."

"I became ill on the ice. Too much skating in circles I suspect. The earl was a perfect gentleman. He saw me to my room, made certain my cousin was with us, and withdrew," Sophie said, chin high.

Lady Bellachat sniffed again, adding a harumph before toddling over to her favorite chair. *Disappointed*, Belinda thought.

"See. It is as I said. There is no call for gossip about Lord Ridgemont. None at all," Dinah Beckwith announced to the room.

Unlike the old biddies who enjoy any scandal broth, Dinah, at least, prefers that Conlyn—Ridgemont—not be caught in a marriage trap. Unless, of course, it was hers. Relief for Sophie's sake calmed Bel when it appeared that oil had been poured on troubled waters.

She slipped from the room. As always, no one took notice.

The kitchen was at sixes and sevens. Mrs. Wesley had taken to her bed—or, Bel suspected, taken a bottle of Uncle Hartwell's claret to her bed—unable to cope with Aunt Violet's threats, the day's menu, or her excitable staff.

Bel rolled up her sleeves, sat the kitchen helpers down, and reviewed the day's plans. It is hard but not impossible to ruin breakfast, but Annie had managed a creditable job on her own. *Thank goodness.* Bel laid out tasks needed for the rest of the day, a timeline, and assignments. Organization always brought calm. Annie, for her part, nodded and asked intelligent questions. Bel had hopes for that one.

Soon carrots were being chopped for the evening's Soup a la Crécy while Annie kneaded two days' supply of bread. Meanwhile, the pot boy assisted in toasting three-day old bread for the mid-day meal. A bit of cheese and ham and it would do for now.

Freed from the need to direct staff, Bel surveyed supplies in the cold closet, mulling what she might do with a leg of lamb and some minced pork. Fish appeared in short supply.

"The glazed lamb three nights ago was superb. You might consider making it again."

The deep voice rumbled through Bel's middle, causing warmth to spread in every direction. Her face burned, and her nether regions tingled strangely. She froze with her back to the man, breathing deeply to settle herself. She couldn't, not as long as she felt his warmth along her back and breathed in his scent, a musky mix of pine and male. *How close is he?*

Bel took a step deeper into the cold closet and turned. Ridgemont stared down at her, and neither spoke for a moment.

"We need to talk. Privately. Shall we walk in the kitchen garden?"

Bel's eyes darted around his side to the kitchen maids. *So much to do…* vied with *How can I escape.*

As if reading her mind he said, "You have plenty of time to prepare dinner."

"No! I—"

He tipped his chin and raised a haughty eyebrow, daring her to lie about her cooking. She didn't. Neither did she move. He was in the way and—she really didn't want to hear what he had to say.

He took her elbow in a grip that felt gentle, until she tried to shake it off and couldn't, and pulled her from the cold closet.

Annie peered at his grip on Bel's elbow with alarm. "Miss Westcott?"

"It will be fine, Annie. Take charge," Bel choked, tripping along with him.

"Miss Westcott and I are going to take a stroll in the garden," Ridgemont said over his shoulder. "She'll return to you soon enough—unharmed. I don't want to interfere with tonight's certain-to-be-delicious dinner." His smile didn't reach his eyes.

He grabbed a cloak from a peg, dragged her out, and slammed the door.

Chapter 8

JOHN ADJUSTED his long stride when Miss Westcott—
Belinda— stumbled just outside the door, but he didn't let
go her arm until they were through the herb garden and
well out of earshot of the kitchen. He stopped by the
chicken house where there was little chance anyone would
see them.

The air had remained crisp and cold, and snow still
covered the ground. She gave herself a shake, peering
around frantically while he wrapped the woolen cloak
around her shoulders, tying it securely at her chin. When
his hands, pressed against the cloak, lingered at her neck
longer than needed, she said nothing.

A man could get lost in this woman's deep blue eyes, he mused.
If he thought to see fear, he saw only confusion. His throat
tightened at the sight. "You must know you need to explain
yourself," he said hoarsely.

Her gaze sharpened, and she straightened before
pulling her eyes from his. "You demanded this conversation. Explain what exactly?"

"Why did you poison the cocoa? You didn't mean to harm your cousin."

She glared at him sharply. "Certainly not! I love Sophie. And it wasn't poison."

"But you don't deny you tainted the drink?"

Her cheeks, already pink with exasperation and cold, turned a deeper red. She dropped her gaze to her feet. Her voice trembled. "No." On a sharp indrawn breath, her head bobbed back up. "I don't make a habit of it, you know!"

He barked an unwilling laugh. "I should think not."

Again, she seemed to find her slippers fascinating.

He lifted her chin with one knuckle. "If you are trying to tell me you had nothing to do with the fiasco two years ago, I already know that."

Stunned surprise made those glorious blue eyes widen. "How do you know?"

"Your cousin Cecil bragged about it."

"Of course, he did, the devil-spawn scum! I was certain he did it. How could he resist boasting?" She turned away, her jaw clenched and her shoulders tight. "You've known all along? Why call me a menace. You were part of the prank!"

"No!" He swallowed hard. "I heard about it late that night. Cecil described it in painful detail. Please believe me. I broke with Cecil's circle of degenerates the next morning."

That seemed to surprise her. "You disappeared soon after. Cecil did too. He left me in peace last Season—he never even came to London. Neither did you. I think the Marquis of Aldridge had something to do with Cecil's departure. I heard him shouting at Uncle Hartwell. The next thing I knew, Cecil was dispatched to Uncle's cottage near Aberdeen. Did he—"

"Banish me? No. My grandfather called me home and there was mourning and—" He waved a hand. "Never mind that. Just answer one thing. You put emetics in that chocolate. You meant it for me, didn't you?" He thought she would look away then, but she did not.

She held his gaze directly. "Yes."

"Why me?"

"If it went up in Cecil's tea that morning, he'd have blamed it on the previous night's excess. It needed to be public just as the other was public."

"Why now? It has been two years."

"Cecil told me you were the one to call me The Westcott Menace."

John grimaced. "I'd deny that if I could. I was so drunk that night I hardly remember anything I said. He may be right, and I sincerely, deeply apologize. The whole distasteful episode shames me. I have never, ever, used that despicable name in public."

"Well, it humiliated me. It still does. He plans to make that public during the next Season. While you are society's darling, the most eligible man in the land, he'll make certain every gossip, every dragon of the Ton, every ambitious mother knows that the Earl of Ridgemont, pearl among pearls, named me a menace."

John felt his blood freeze in his veins one moment only to boil the next as rage consumed him. His curses would have shocked an army sergeant. They seemed to amuse Belinda Westcott.

"I take it that is news to you," she said.

"Of course, it is. I would have nothing to do with a scheme to humiliate you."

She stepped away. "Thank you for that, at least. I need to go back in now. Dinner won't prepare itself.

"I'm glad no permanent harm came to Lady Sophie. I

wish I had never handed her that mug. She's lucky to have you; you took excellent care of her."

She whispered thanks and walked away.

Excellent care... John suspected everyone at Hartwell Hall benefitted from Belinda Westcott's care. As he watched her graceful, determined stride, attraction heated him. He thought of her cooking and smiled. Belinda Westcott was the one woman at this benighted house party interesting enough to pursue, or at least worth further acquaintance. First, however, he needed to confront Cecil Hartwell. The worm.

BEL WANDERED into the kitchen in a daze, absently sniffing the broth simmering on the hob. *Ridgemont apologized. He wasn't privy to Cecil's mischief, and yet he apologized for his part.* Ridgemont was not at all the man she thought he was. He treated Sophie with respect. He went back to check on the others. He... He apologized to Bel. No one ever did that. Certainly, no man ever did.

"Is all well, Miss?" Annie's question snapped Bel out of her abstraction. The girl's worried expression brought her back to business.

"Glazed lamb tonight, I think," she said, removing the cloak, memories of the hands that had so gently placed it on her shoulders haunting her. She put them away just as she put the cloak on its peg. "We still have dried apricots to go with the sugar syrup."

Breathing a collective sigh of relief, the entire kitchen hummed productively, and the afternoon sped by.

She wasn't certain later how she managed to dress for dinner on time to join guests in the drawing room. She endured the meal with great effort, placed as she was between Lady Arncastle and Mr. Barnstable the vicar, who was slightly deaf. Lady Arncastle sniffed every dish while eyeing Bel suspiciously. Cecil sat across from her three places down, and the sneer he sent her way seemed particularly menacing.

Worse, she struggled to keep her mind from Ridgemont, and her glance from wandering his way. She chided herself not to act like a schoolgirl, but could not seem to control it. *Curiosity. That's what it is. Curiosity*, she told herself. *Just get through dinner.* She disciplined her mind to think only about the service and general reactions of the guests to her cooking and decided she would retire as soon as the ladies withdrew.

But then Uncle announced that, since card games were planned for the evening, the gentlemen would forego their port and join the ladies. Cecil commandeered the bottle and trooped out after uncle. Bel shuddered.

"He won't misbehave in front of his father. At least one hopes not." She turned to see Ridgemont offering his arm. She took it; warm pleasure flowed through her at the touch and all thoughts of hiding away upstairs evaporated.

What is going on with you, Bel?

"You frowned, Miss Westcott. Do you not enjoy cards?" he asked.

"I sometimes enjoy whist," she stuttered.

They had reached the music salon where tables had been set up for cards. "Would you prefer to take a turn around the room and observe?"

The urge to follow him anywhere startled her. She couldn't formulate a reply.

"Or perhaps a walk in the garden?" His intense gaze scattered her thoughts.

"Alone?" she croaked.

A grin, slow and sensual, transformed his face. "Perhaps not. Shall we take tea then?" He nodded toward a settee along the side between the tea table and the pianoforte that had been pushed to the side. One with room for two and no one else. Private in the midst of company.

Bel studied it briefly. The moment she raised her head to look at him, a smile filled her entire being. He wasn't the horrid man she thought. He was the catch of the Season. And he sought her company. "I would like that very much," she said.

She couldn't say later, alone in her bed, what happened between them. They never did play cards, despite hints from Aunt Violet, Sophie, and even from Lady Bellachat. Dinah Beckwith's comments were even more pointed, but Ridgemont—John—ignored them.

They spoke of mundane things. Her lonely childhood in a house of scholars. His favorite pony. Boyhood pranks. Books they liked and ones they didn't. Mutual acquaintances. His education. Her struggles over its lack and efforts to educate herself. None of it was intimate and yet…

As the company began to disperse, everyone seemed to stare at her. She didn't care. John's last words were to ask her to walk out with him tomorrow. She would. Even icy rain wouldn't keep her from it.

Chapter 9

THE STINK of cigar and spilled spirits wafted under the door to the billiard room accompanied by raucous laughter and the punchline to a particularly vulgar story. John's nose wrinkled, recoiling, but he pushed the door open with grim determination

Harry Smithers struck the table with his cue, ripping the covering and sending his ball bouncing across the room. The other players doubled over in inane hilarity, as if Harry's clumsiness was amusing rather than destructive. Another aging adolescent snored where he lay on his side in the corner while a fourth puked into a potted fern. Bottles lay strewn across the floor.

How can the earl and countess tolerate this boorish behavior? John slammed the door behind him. "Where is Lord Cecil," he demanded.

"Oy, Ridgemont. Finally come to play?" Smithers grinned. "Best find a drink." He gestured, swayed, and almost lost his footing. "We're way ahead of you."

"I asked a question. Where is Cecil?"

"D'you know, Edwards?" Smithers asked the man by the fern, still green around the gills.

"Wen' out. Hadda piss." The man swayed and dropped to his seat on the floor.

The French doors were slightly ajar. John made his way cautiously across the floor and out. The billiard room was located in the farthest reaches of the house facing the back, probably so the countess could avoid knowing what went on. It opened out on to a flagstone terrace with a few mismatched chairs with rattan seats.

Cecil stood at the end relieving himself into a rose bush.

"You're so uncouth I am surprised you spare your mother's carpet," John growled. He stood in the pool of light from the billiard room.

Cecil staggered toward him.

"All high and mighty now you're heir. Did you poison your cousin to get it?" Cecil sneered, leaning on the wall for support.

"You have a fixation with sickening people one way or another, Hartwell." John glanced at the degenerates in the billiard room. "I heard your parents sent you to some patch of land in Scotland to rusticate. Looks like they let you back too soon."

"'S my home, Ridgemont. Leave if you don't like it."

I wouldn't have come if I knew you were here.

"You threatened Miss Westcott." It was a flat statement.

"What if I did? She deserves it. 'S 'er fault I've been dying of boredom for a year or more. Been a snitch since she earned me a birching from our grandfather. Grew up an unfeminine bluestocking bitch."

John had Cecil's cravat in a punishing grip before he could blink. The reprobate gagged and flailed his hands about in an attempt to loosen the suffocating hold. John threw him against the wall, and Cecil bent double gasping for air, his attacker looming over him.

"You threatened an innocent—"

"Bel ain't no innocent miss. She gives as good as she gets," Cecil, bent over, rasped between breaths.

"And you attached my name to your vile insults."

"You mean the Menace business? You came up with it. Damn good name," Cecil muttered, coming upright. "Thought she oughta know," he sneered.

John loomed closer. "Miss Westcott received my apologies graciously enough. I regret every moment I spent with you and your band of foulmouthed sycophants that year."

"Now you're heir you're better than us? Watch you don't blot your copybook with the patronesses and dragons. A word or two and—

Cecil's feet left the floor when John dragged him up by his filthy cravat. "Show your face in London during the Season, and whatever Aldridge threatened will be nothing compared to what I will do to you."

Cecil fell to the floor gulping for air.

"Perhaps I will have a quiet word with your father and tell him so."

BEL SWEPT the curtains in her room aside as dawn broke, spreading golden light across the snow. Looking forward to the day and the promised walk, she was anxious to get breakfast on its way. She picked up one of the plain grey gowns she preferred for the kitchen and dropped it. Not today.

Not long after, she entered the kitchen in a printed muslin day dress, light brown covered in tiny rosettes. She had tucked an unbleached lace fichu at her neck on impulse at the last moment.

"You look extra fine this morning, Miss," Annie exclaimed. "Have you done something new with your hair?"

"Not really. I was just tired of the bun in back." Without Susan she couldn't create a fashionable do, but she had brushed her brown curls into an upsweep held up with a band around her head. "Let's try Chelsea buns this morning, shall we?" She asked, blushing and covering her dress with an apron.

Soon, dough lay rising, currents plumped in brandy, and the tweeny entered with the morning's eggs while Bel cooked kippers and Annie prepared filling for the buns.

"I knew you would be up early!" At the sound of John's voice Bel's entire body came alert. "Let's have that walk now before the eyes and ears awaken," he continued.

John snatched a pinch of currents from the bowl, laughing when Bel smacked his hand.

"My grandmother's cook always did the same," he said. "Shall we go? It looks like you have things well underway."

"You go, Miss. I can handle breakfast, truly," Annie said, smiling back and forth between Bel and John.

Bel hesitated.

"Do you want a maid to follow us?" he asked.

Thoughtful and kind. She brushed his suggestion aside. She was beyond needing a chaperone. Besides, as he said, they were up before snooping eyes and ears. "Nonsense. I'm not some dewy-eyed young miss. Annie, please take over while I take a brief walk with Lord Ridgemont."

She'd worn sturdy boots that morning, and brought her own warm cloak and bonnet downstairs. Soon enough they were on their way, and he led her toward the woodlot.

He said nothing until they were well past the kitchen gardens. "I need to ask questions you may not want to answer in front of other people."

What on earth could he want? Panic filled her. He didn't seem to notice.

"Tell me, Miss Westcott, have you always been your aunts' cook?"

She laughed in relief. "Only Aunt Violet's. She pretends I'm only supervising. Aunt Flora—Marchioness of Gilford—won't let me near the kitchen. She's determined that I must be a proper debutante, even after six Seasons."

"Why do you do it?" He wrinkled his brow.

"It makes me happy," she answered simply, unwilling to expand on that.

"You are certainly an excellent chef. I would rate some of your dishes as equal to fine meals I've had in Paris and Vienna."

Her heart warmed at the flattery but sank at the next question.

"What about it makes you happy?"

"I like creating something admired by people, even if none of them know I'm the one doing it. The creative process intrigues me," she replied.

"Intrigues you how?" he asked.

Bel's nerves settled in the face of his genuine interest.

"Combining ingredients in various ways, with various spices and flavorings results in different—sometimes surprising—results. It is a kind of practical chemistry," she said before she thought about her words.

"Chemistry?" he pounced on the word.

Bel breathed deeply and came to a decision. Honesty mattered. Better sooner than later. "I find chemistry fascinating." She shot a glance at him. "When Mr. Davy speaks—"

"Sir Humphry Davy? You've attended his lectures?" He couldn't keep shock from his voice.

Bel stiffened her resolve. "Yes, and not, as the gossips say, because ladies are drawn to his looks. His lectures were the closest I could come to university lectures. I went whenever I could get away from my aunts. His accident with nitrogen trichloride was such a tragedy. I would never attempt such a thing."

"You've attempted other experiments." It wasn't a question; he studied her closely.

"I keep a laboratory outside Aunt Violet's kitchen. It's one reason I like it here."

"But how marvelous! My grandfather will love you."

His grandfather? She stopped her steps and turned to peer into his face. His hazel eyes held hers spellbound. She looked away first and resumed walking, unable to manage the intensity any longer. "And what of you?" she asked. "I bared my soul. Can you do the same? What were you doing in London that spring, in Cecil's circle of all things?

"I was invalided home from Spain where I had contracted camp fever. They didn't expect me to live, and even when I came to, I could not shake it. They sent me home to recuperate. Effects lingered."

"You were in the military? I must have known that, but somehow—"

"I didn't act much like a soldier. I hardly left the bottom of a brandy bottle that spring, so discouraged was I to be so weak. All I wanted was to rejoin my regiment. The army was my life."

"But you never went back!" She swung around to look at him, and they paused in the shelter of the trees.

"No," he said softly. "I was called to the family estate."

She struggled to choose words carefully. "It is never good news when a family member dies, even if one benefits."

"My cousin, alas, was not a good man and wasn't seriously mourned. But benefits? It didn't feel like it. The weight of the family, the estate, and the lives of many fell on me. I was some months adjusting. But there was Grandfather, encouraging me."

"Your father had preceded him?"

"My parents died when I was sixteen. I lived with my grandparents briefly before I convinced Grandfather to buy me colors. My father's older brother and his son still lived. Grandfather let me go because I wasn't close to the succession."

"I'm so sorry for your losses," she murmured studying his face.

"Don't be. Reacquainting with the old gentleman has been a joy. I always knew I had their love and respect, but it was a distant thing. I didn't know the extent to which I missed having family near."

Her throat felt thick and moisture pooled in her eyes, to her consternation, yet she couldn't look away.

"And now I know I must form one of my own. Grandfather instructed me to find a lady of character and ability. One with the strength to be my partner in what is coming when I inherit. Pedigree, he believes, matters little." John laughed lightly. "He growled that those 'fools in the Ton wouldn't know quality if it bit them.' He was never much for London society, though he encourages me to navigate it cautiously. He only goes down for parliamentary affairs."

His intense gaze sent her emotions into a maelstrom. The moment stretched unbearably until Bel had to break away. She took two steps when an impulse struck. She leaned over, scooped up a handful of snow and hit him square in the chest with a snowball.

"I heard you were a deft hand with snow the other day," she challenged holding her breath and immediately regretted it. She gasped at John's predatory expression.

Bel, you damned fool. That was a reckless way to deflect an uncomfortable moment. She broke into a run, but wasn't fast enough.

John didn't hesitate. He prowled in her direction with two hands full of snow. Icy cold hit the back of her neck and dripped under her cloak. The other handful went down her chin. She scrambled to pick up another handful, but he reached her quickly with more.

The two of them wrestled with each other, laughing like fools, painting one another with snow, until Bel slipped on her cloak and fell over pulling John with her. They lay tangled, Bel on her back, John over her.

While they stared at each other, Bel surreptitiously scooped a handful of snow at her side.

No slow-top, he clamped his hand on her wrist forcing her to drop it. "Clever tactic, Miss Westcott. Wellington would admire it." He kissed her lightly. "Unsuccessful though," he murmured kissing her again."

"Was it?" she asked, kissing him back. "That depends on my intention, don't you think."

He kissed her again, sliding his tongue along her mouth, seeking entrance. When she gave it, all coherent thought fled. He kissed his way along her chin to the spot below her ear, and Bel's body felt as if it burst into flames. She ran her fingers through his thick hair, pulling him close until his mouth returned to hers and his clever hands began to explore her beneath the cloak.

When John started to move away, she groaned and tried to pull him back. "Why Miss Westcott, delightful as this is, I best stop while I still have some claim to the name gentleman."

Startled back to reality, Bel started to protest, but good sense suggested better. She let him help her to her feet, not meeting his eyes. She patted and shook her cloak to remove the snow.

"You know, Miss Westcott, I do believe you have snowed me completely," John laughed, knocking the melting stuff from his clothing. The movement of his hands along his trousers and his cheeky grin sent bolts of heat through her whole body, melted her frozen knees and robbed her of speech.

"Shall we go back while we have only your kitchen friends to face?" he asked.

Her hand trembled when she took his arm. He started to speak, but she shook her head. He ignored her. "I apologize if my behavior offended, but I rather think you enjoyed it. If you don't wish to speak of it now, fine, but we will. We must."

Chapter 10

BEL SOUGHT refuge in the kitchen, her place of comfort, her emotions a seething mass of confusion, mortification, and delight over what passed between her and Ridgemont.

With breakfast finished and preparation for the midday nuncheon well underway, Bel poured herself tea and sat at the battered kitchen table to rest. *What in the name of all that's holy just happened?*

She closed her eyes and let the fine China tea warm her, her thoughts in a muddle. *The wretch wants to 'talk about' what passed between us?* She took another sip and gave herself a mental shake. *Since when are you a coward, Bel? What do you want to make of it? Where do you hope it will lead? Another woman would have a betrothal in hand after that assault.*

Another sip. *Assault? Don't be a ninny. You were laughing and having fun one minute, and kissing him as if your life depended on it the next. Perhaps it does.*

She shook off that bit of drama and poured more tea. She pretended not to see the sly glances Annie and the others shot her way periodically, and the notice they took of her wet cloak. The girls seemed to ponder whether Bel had become overwhelmed with joy or out of sorts with Lord Ridgemont. She couldn't have told them.

Annie shyly brought her a plate of Chelsea buns. "You look distressed, Miss, and you missed breakfast."

Bel smiled at the girl. "Not distressed, Annie, merely thinking something through."

It was true she realized. Nothing he had said or done distressed her. She simply wasn't sure what it meant. *If something puzzles me in the kitchen or the lab, I analyze it, sort out the variables and perhaps experiment. That's what I ought to be doing. Listing the possibilities.*

Two buns later a thought struck her. *Was that kiss an experiment? If so, what did I learn?* Bel was too honest not to admit that one thing she learned was that she liked kissing Ridgemont, liked it very much.

She shook off her abstraction to oversee midday nuncheon. The work distracted her as it always did. Time flew until the footmen arrived, and she gave serving instructions. "Is everything ready in the large drawing room?"

"Yes, Miss. Exactly as you instructed. You'll see when you come up," George said cheerfully.

I can't. Damn. Aunt Violet expected her at meals. *I can't face Ridgemont until I know what to say to him. Not Ridgemont. John. Horsefeathers. I don't even know what to call him.*

"Kindly inform Lady Hartwell that I am indisposed."

George raised an impertinent eyebrow, but he bowed and said he would.

The chaos of nuncheon settled before she remembered one other thing.

She had promised Sophie she would turn pages while her cousin practiced for the musicale planned for the evening. Sophie urged her to sing, and she had been tempted. How could she possibly face Sophie after rolling in the snow with that man? It would show on her face—it must—and she couldn't possibly explain.

No, I won't. I'll simply ignore—

"I knew I'd find you here. Aunt Violet said you were indisposed, but you weren't in your room. What are you playing at, Bel?" Sophie stood, arms akimbo, right in front of Bel.

Bel suppressed her groan. "Annie, I need a moment with my cousin. Kindly take the others and assist the footmen tidying up."

Sophie's look of concern intensified at that. "Tell me," she demanded as soon as they were alone.

Bel hesitated.

"The truth," Sophie folded her arms at her waist and glared at Bel.

"John... That is, Lord Ridgemont kissed me."

Sophie's expressive face transformed from confusion to disbelief to pure delight in the space of three heartbeats. "But that's, that's—"

"I don't know what it is, perhaps nothing," Bel said.

"Nothing? Is that what you want?"

"I don't know what I want."

"A simple kiss is nothing to fret about. I had three rather nice ones last season." Sophie's cheeks went pink at that, and Bel realized how innocent her cousin truly was. Innocent but not ignorant.

"It wasn't simple. It was well beyond 'rather nice.' Sophie! We rolled on the ground!"

Sophie gasped so hard she choked, and struggled for breath. "If Aunt Violet hears that she'll have you at the altar tomorrow—or however long it takes to fetch a license."

Bel tried to find words to explain. She hesitated so long Sophie looked alarmed.

"Didn't you like it?" Sophie demanded. "Did Ridgemont… That is, did he force you?"

"Good grief no! I liked it very well. Too much. That's the problem. He is too honorable a man to be forced into marriage by a momentary lapse."

Sophie relaxed at that. "Will you accept if he offers?"

That's what I'm trying to sort out… Suddenly there was nothing to sort. Bel knew exactly what she wanted.

"If John could convince me that marriage is what he truly wants, that he isn't being coerced by some pompous male honor, then yes. I expect I would accept. But how can he? We've known each other less than a week."

Sophie's expression turned sly and the sides of her mouth lifted. "John, is it?"

Bel blushed. "Ridgemont sounds a bit formal under the circumstances."

The kitchen maids trooped in after the footman and the cart of dirty dishes.

"Enough, Sophie! We have work to do."

Sophie glanced around and nodded at Bel. "Will I see you at dinner?"

"Yes. Perhaps. If I can get control of what I need to say," Bel murmured.

"I'll cover for you with Aunt Violet, but you have to face him eventually."

JOHN TRUDGED into his rooms and marched toward the dressing room trailing water.

Graves frowned in disapproval. "What have ye done to yerself? Y'look like y've rolled in the snow."

John shot him a scathing look.

"You did! Y'walked out with a fine lady and come

home wet from the snow. Yer grandfather will have your head if y'don't—"

"I know my duty, Graves. Just help me change clothes."

The valet did so in sullen silence.

When John requested an evening coat, Grave's eyebrow rose. The valet took an inordinate amount of time with the cravat. "Get on with it, man!" John spat.

"If yer speaking with the earl you best look the part of a fine gentleman," Graves muttered.

"I'm not…" Well, in fact he did plan to speak with the Earl of Hartwell but not for the reason Graves assumed. At least not yet.

John went down to the breakfast room, searching for Bel as soon as he entered, only to be disappointed. They needed to sort through what was happening between them. He needed to know how she felt, but she wasn't there. Neither were Cecil and his group, thank goodness, but it was much too early for them to arise. Neither was Lord Hartwell, unfortunately.

John would have to wait, something he loathed doing. He retired to the library while the ladies fluttered to the drawing room and some of the younger men set off on a morning ride. He spent two hours alternately sifting through newspapers and pacing the library. All he could think about was his behavior with Bel. He'd crossed the line a gentleman should not cross. The trouble was he wanted to do it again—and more. He couldn't get the feel of her out of his head.

Finally, certain he would go mad waiting, he prowled the first floor searching for Hartwell. Searching for Bel. To no avail. When she failed to turn up for nuncheon, he knew she was hiding from him. The meal had such a fine touch he knew where to find her, but he restrained himself from storming the kitchen. If Bel needed time, he would give it to her.

At least, the earl had risen and joined his guests at last. John waited impatiently for the meal to finish. As it wound down, Peter Hartley suggested to some others that they seek the billiard room.

"I wouldn't. I saw it last night, and the surface of the table has been damaged," John told him quietly. The earl heard the exchange and frowned. When he approached, John didn't give him a chance to question his comment about billiards. Before the earl could speak, John asked for a private word. Unfortunately, Lady Bellachat overheard and sent him a smug look. Peter Hartley saw it and grinned at him.

Dear God, gossip already. I really do need to speak with Bel.

The earl's study smelled of smoke and beeswax, far better than the aromas his son's friends left in their wake. They sat in leather chairs with a small table between them. Hartwell didn't offer him a drink. He could have used one.

"What do you have to say to me? Something happy, I hope." Hartwell began.

Can he think I mean to offer for his niece already?

"No." At John's curt response the earl's eyes flew wide. "I need to discuss your son."

"My son? See here, Ridgemont! My family is none of your business."

"Ordinarily, that is true. However ill-behaved Cecil is, he is your problem, not mine. When he insults me and threatens to shame my good name, it becomes my problem. Do you even know what he has been up to?"

"I have a feeling you plan to tell me," the older man said, sinking back.

"I understand you had words with the Marquis of Aldridge the season before last."

"Aldridge? That was…" the earl sputtered

John held up a staying hand. "He accused Cecil of causing the disaster at The Duchess of Haverford's venetian breakfast and blaming it on Miss Westcott. He was correct. I know because Cecil bragged about it. In detail. He was proud of what he did to those people and particularly proud of making a fool of B— Miss Westcott."

"He never did like her," Hartwell muttered. "But how is it an insult to you?"

"I am ashamed to tell you that I was drunk that night. When they began a round of making up foolish names for the lady—The Westcott Witch, Bel the Bilious, The Westcott Assassin, The Westcott Fiend—laughing every time. I muttered "The Westcott Menace," they howled, and it stuck. I never intended to harm the lady; I never said the foul name again. Cecil did. He spread it far and wide."

"So I was told, and we sent him away. It died down when the Season ended. One didn't hear a word of it last year."

"I gathered that. I assume he was invited back this week for that reason."

The earl shrugged and John went on. "This week he is at it again. Cecil told B— erm, Miss Westcott that, when he returns to London in the Spring, he plans to spread the hateful nickname far and wide and make certain society learns I am the culprit who made it up. It won't do me any harm, but it will your niece. Cecil thinks it will hurt her more if the catch of the Season—his words not mine— thinks she's a menace."

The earl closed his eyes and sighed deeply. "He didn't learn anything."

"No, he did not. Perhaps I should explain what I said to Peter. I went in search of Cecil and found your billiard room stinking of smoke, brandy and vomit and afloat in bottles and unmentionable stains. Harry Smithers destroyed the surface of the table just as I walked in. They found it hilarious. The bunch of them are worthless juvenile trouble makers. I suggest you exile him again and forbid his friends to follow."

The earl nodded sadly. "I hoped allowing him home as his mother begged would show him improved. Not so. There won't be much left of our good name for David to inherit if he continues unchecked."

"I'm sorry to bear bad news," John murmured.

"I'm glad you did. It is as I feared. His mother refuses to hear it, but she'll have to bear it." The earl laughed bitterly. "And here I thought you wanted to speak of my niece."

"Not quite yet."

"With Cecil's behavior I can hardly blame you, but Sophie is a fine girl."

Sophie? Is he mad? "Lady Sophie is a lovely girl, but not my interest."

The earl jerked upright. "Bel? You are interested in Bel?"

"Interested yes, but not decided. We've known each other but a week, and the lady has had a difficult time of it. She needs time to get to know me."

The earl nodded. "A good girl is Bel, but she has an odd hitch or two to her step that hasn't served her well."

"Do I have your permission to court the lady? Perhaps in time I'll come to her guardians for permission to offer for her."

The earl smiled then, genuinely pleased. "Bel deserves happiness. I wouldn't have thought she was the sort you'd want, though. Treat her gently. Don't break her heart."

"You may count on it," John replied.

After that, the afternoon crawled. When Bel didn't turn up for dinner, he had had enough.

As soon as the gentlemen finished their port, he paused in the hallway, torn between retiring and seeking her out.

"She's in the kitchen, of course."

He turned to see Lady Sophie with an impish grin. "Go talk to her.

Chapter 11

AFTER A DAY of seething emotion Bel retreated into the thing that focused her mind in times of trouble, her laboratory. The tiny room had once been the kitchen buttery; its outside wall made of stone. The door hung open, and the kitchen behind her was wrapped in darkness and silence, but the oil lamps that hung on either side of her gave off just enough light.

Bel held a vial of nitrate of silver with great care. It was her fifth effort to study the effects of it on various substances, and she was running out. Holding the vial steady, she lowered a thin sliver of copper into it. She had scavenged the copper from the frame Aunt Flora had given her to hold her mother's miniature. The damaged corner of the frame was a pity, but needs must. She got her material where she could.

"Bel!"

A voice stopped her breath and made her heart race. She peered over her shoulder to see John walking toward her in the shadows, a wry smile on his face. She half turned still holding the vial and caught sight of a blur behind him.

Before she could think, John crashed into her, the door to the laboratory slammed shut, and her vial shattered on the floor. A key turned in the lock.

What on earth?

"You spiked my plans for Spring, so I spiked yours." Cecil growled at them, kicking the thick door. The sound of his footsteps stomping away was followed by total silence.

John's warm body pressed up against hers, robbing Bel of coherent thought. His arms came around her and slid up her back, cradling her closely. There being little room to move, she leaned her forehead into his shoulder, savoring the piney smell he always brought with him. "Did I hurt you?" John murmured.

She shook her head, still against his shoulder. "Cecil again. What did he mean I spiked his plans?"

"Not you. Me. I had a word with the earl. I suspect your nasty cousin has been banished back to the wilds of Aberdeenshire," he replied rubbing circles on her back.

"Good!" she said fiercely. She backed up an inch or two, enough to look down at the floor. Her precious nitrate of silver was destroyed. "Drat him. That was the last of it."

"What was it?" John asked, peering around the tiny room for the first time.

"Nitrate of silver," she replied.

"Saints and the devil protect us! That stuff is dangerous."

Bel pointed upward with her chin toward the grillwork, ten or eleven inches high, that lined the outside wall just below the ceiling. "There is ventilation. I'm not a complete fool. Though I admit, I usually work with substances like that on my table in the chicken house."

"This is a chemistry laboratory!"

Bel grinned up at him. "Clever of you to notice."

"I thought it was some sort of herbal apothecary," he grumbled.

She ignored him and surveyed the floor. "It's probably best if I cover it though. Help me remove my smock." She untied the bow at her neck.

John brushed her hands away and slid the smock down her arms, and the sensation of his hands along the soft muslin of her gown sent shivers through her. "Where on earth did you get nitrate of silver?" he asked.

She set about covering the mess on the floor with her smock. At his question she peered up and sighed. "I mostly order supplies from members of Apothecaries' Hall in London, when I can afford it from my pin money. I have them sent here, care of M.R. Wesley, and the cook takes possession for me. Nitrate of silver is too dear, so I made my own."

"Made your own?!"

She had truly astonished him now, and it delighted her. "Nitric acid was easy enough to obtain. I just hope Aunt Flora doesn't notice I no longer wear the silver chain for the cross my father gave me. I put it on a velvet ribbon."

"I hope you did that in the chicken coop," he grumbled.

Bel grinned. "I did. With mask and gloves. Speaking of which…" she pulled off her kid gloves and dropped them on the table behind her.

John shook his head. "You are remarkable."

A surge of pride overwhelmed Bel. No one had ever called her remarkable before. Peculiar, strange, or horrid, but never remarkable. "I might be if I had a real laboratory with good storage for problematic chemicals. And proper ventilation."

His smile melted her insides. "I have no doubt you would be. You continue to astonish me more every time we speak." His words cast a spell, binding her eyes to his. They stood chest to chest, eyes fixed together, as if enveloped in a realm in which no words were needed, a kingdom of their own vibrating with attraction and desire.

John moved eventually, lowering his head with infinite care, giving her every chance to protest, while Bel gripped his shoulders, unable to move. The kiss, when it came, radiated joy and a sense of inevitability. The feel of his mouth on her drew her deeper and deeper into a new world of joy, one in which only the two of them existed. She would have allowed him anything.

"We need to stop this." His voice sounded miles away; Bel raised up on tiptoe to recapture his mouth with hers, and he joined his lips to hers, if only for a moment. "Bel, we're locked in. We need to get out," he murmured.

Bell came down to earth; reality, cold and brutal, lashed her. She blinked to clear her head.

"I'm sorry," she whispered.

"Whatever for?" he asked.

HOW LONG HAS *this treasure of a woman been taking blame for all disasters large and small?*

John cupped Bel's face with gentle hands. "You have nothing to apologize for. This is another mess of Cecil's making. I rather liked what just passed between us, and I believe you did to. As delightful as it would be to continue, it won't do. You must know that."

Bel sighed, closed her eyes, but made no attempt to move out of his arms. "Cecil means for us to be found together. He's trying to force you into an unwanted marriage."

"Are you certain it would be unwanted?" he asked

Her eyes flew open, wide in astonishment at the question. "We've only known each other a few days! I'll not have you forced, when they all know you can have anyone you want come Spring."

"And if I want you?"

She held her peace, leaving John more downcast than he expected. Her words about short acquaintance were correct, however. "You don't want to be forced, either. I can see that."

She shook her head. "Let's see if we can get out of here, and ruin Cecil's plots. We'll worry about the rest if we fail."

With effort in the narrow space, they rearranged their position so they both faced the door. John tried the handle, which proved what they already assumed. The door was firmly locked.

"I don't suppose you know how to pick the lock," Bel mused pulling out one of her hair pins.

"I'm hoping you do," he said.

She peered at the hairpin. "I've heard of people managing with one of these, but I have no idea how."

John shrugged. "We can try it." He bent the pin and knelt in front of the lock. Bel's hand on his shoulder made him wish to be a hero, but alas, the lock proved recalcitrant. It would not budge. He rose to face her. "I'm sorry Bel. Failure."

"At least you tried. We could call for help, I suppose." She sounded doubtful.

"They wouldn't hear us down here. Even if they did, it would bring the gossips down on you, and the wrath of the earl down on me. We should avoid that if we can."

"Annie and the others will rise by five to start the kitchen fires. They'll let us out and won't gossip," she said.

John could think of nothing he'd like more than spending a night with Bel, but not in a tiny closet stinking of chemicals. "Servants gossip worse than their mistresses."

Her sad smile cut him to the heart. "Not these. I have their loyalty."

He pulled her back into his arms, and set her head against his shoulder. With the closed door cutting off the kitchen warmth, Bel's "ventilation" had rapidly dropped the temperature. "We'll freeze if we stay here."

"I'm feeling nicely warm right now," she said, her words muffled against his coat. She glanced up with mischief in her eyes. "We could keep each other warm."

Her suggestion sent lascivious images floating through his imagination. As delightful as that appeared, it wouldn't suffice. Sooner or later, they would fall asleep, freeze, or be sickened by the chemicals, and come to grief.

"What is that grill work made of?" he asked glancing up.

"Wrought iron I think."

"Help me climb up."

"There is a stool under the counter. You can probably stand on it, but be careful," she said.

"If I slip, I'll just fall into your arms." *Right where I want to be.* John grinned at her.

The stool turned out to be sturdy enough. He scrambled up and found he could just reach the grill work, though the counter kept him a bit too far back. "Do you think the counter will hold me?" he asked, peering down at her.

"I have no idea; I never tried standing on it, but it has always been stable."

When he stepped up onto the counter, the bottles on

the narrow shelves shook and clanged together, but the counter held firm under him. Bel put her hands on his legs as if to steady him. "Don't do that, love. It is too distracting," he said imagining other circumstances in which he'd welcome her touch.

"Sorry," she said in a quiet voice, yanking her hands away. "Can you reach it?"

"Yes. Iron for certain but well mortared in. Even if I could budge the grill, I don't think either of us is small enough to wiggle out. He turned and ran a hand around the back of his neck. "Push the stool back under, and I'll jump down."

She did as he asked. "Be—"

He was down before she could finish, sliding down in front of her and pulling her into his arms. He kissed her again, thoroughly this time, claiming her mouth and exploring her lush curves.

She followed where he led for moments, but when she pulled back and gasped for breath, she asked. "What was that for?"

Need. Desire. Want. Frustrated need to protect you. "Warmth," he said kissing her again.

"Bel? Bel where are you." Lady Sophie's voice.

Gratitude flashed through him followed quickly by disappointment. *Damn*, he thought. *I'd have liked a few minutes more.*

Chapter 12

EVERY FIBER in Bel's body vibrated with awareness of John close to her. "Sophie! We're here. We're locked in," she shouted.

"Oh no. Ridgemont is in there with you? I came to warn you," Sophie replied coming close to the locked door.

"How did you know? Never mind—get us out, and we can talk," Bel replied.

"I don't see a key," Sophie said.

"Pray he didn't take it with him," John murmured.

"Wait, here it is on the table. He left it on purpose." Soon the key rattled in the lock.

"What do you mean 'on purpose?'" Bel demanded while she waited.

"Cecil means for you to be found. He set one of the footmen to whisper in Aunt Violet's ear. I heard him in the hall, but when I went out—oh drat! This key is giving me fits, and I don't think we have much time."

"Stay calm, Sophie. Press down on the key as you turn it. It is finicky," Bel told her. The key continued to rattle.

John put his arm around Bel's waist and kissed the top

of her head. "It will come out right," he said. Bel turned her head into his shoulder.

A firm click signaled success. With the lock breached, Sophie opened the door easily. Before they could step out, however, a shout boded disaster.

"What is going on down here at this hour of the night," the Earl of Harwell growled. "And what are you doing here Sophie?"

"Bel," Aunt Violet moaned "Whatever will people say?"

The sight of Lady Ancaster following the noise told Bel all she needed to know about what people might say. "I can explain," she said.

"So can I," Sophie cut in. "Cecil locked them in and then sent a footman to frighten you. Cecil—"

"But what was Ridgemont doing down here in the middle of the night, and what is that room you were in?" Bel's uncle demanded.

"It is my laboratory," Bel said lifting her chin and daring him to criticize.

"In my kitchen?" Aunt Violet shrieked, glancing at Lady Ancaster who had been joined by Viscountess Bellachat tottering on her cane.

Hartwell pinched the bridge of his nose and closed his eyes momentarily before pinning John with a pointed glance. "Ridgemont, we need to talk."

"I'll join you privately whenever you want. First, however, you need to know that Lord Cecil Hartwell has done his best to harass and humiliate this innocent woman for years. I will not have her forced into marriage."

Of course not. He doesn't want to be forced to marry me, Bel thought.

"It is an ungodly hour. You will meet me in the morning," the earl replied. "Bel, get yourself to your room. You too Sophie."

John nodded and took a step toward the circle of gawking witnesses.

"I will, Uncle. As soon as I clean up this mess," Bel said turning to her workbench.

Aunt Violet shook herself, the ruffles of her dressing gown fluttering around her. "You will do no such thing! I will have the servants clean it up and empty it out. Your so-called laboratory will be gone."

Bel opened her mouth to object, but knew it for the hopeless case it was. She walked, head down, past the avidly watching Lady Ancaster.

John came as close as he dared in front of the harpies. She cast him a look, bleak and helpless.

"It will all come right, I promise," he whispered before walking on and leaving her.

Sophie took her hand as they walked to the stairs. Her silent gaze held more sympathy than words could have added.

IMPECCABLY DRESSED, with all of Graves's skill, John took a deep breath and knocked on the Earl of Hartwell's study the next morning as expected. The voices inside were raised, one of them distraught. Bel's aunt wasn't going to make things easy for them.

A fraught half hour later, John was given permission—ordered, in fact—to attend Bel in the small formal parlor. He watched her pacing for a moment before she saw him at the door. She had dressed in a green silk gown flocked with tiny white flowers that flowed in flattering waves across curves now familiar to his touch.

He shut the door, and she turned at the sound. "Tell me you didn't let them bully you," she said breathlessly.

As they bully you? But no, that wasn't entirely true. She wasn't defenseless. Bel had carved out her own haven here with quiet strength. He took both her hands in his and kissed her knuckles. "Come sit."

"Tell me," she insisted when they sat together on the settee.

"Your Aunt and Uncle are understandably concerned about your reputation," he began.

"Concerned? Aunt Violet is in full on collapse over Lady Ancaster."

John smiled. It wasn't inaccurate. "I refused your uncle's insistence we obtain a common license and marry within the week."

"I should hope so! He has no right to force you into that," she said.

"Bel, I will happily marry you, but you deserve better than a havey-cavey wedding that will only feed the gossips. You've been through enough at your cousin's hands. I told him so. Cecil is gone, by the way. Dispatched to the manor in Aberdeenshire on short funds at dawn with two grooms assigned to make sure he gets there. Harry Smithers and the others were sent to the posting inn in the village to make their way to London."

"Well, that is a small blessing. Thank you for insisting we will not wed—and for defending me." Moisture welled in her eyes, but she kept her shoulders and face firmly under control.

Her gratitude at what she saw as his protection left him shaken, wondering how to convince her. "I spoke with the earl yesterday and told him I planned court you properly in the spring. And I will."

"What?"

"And only if you find that we will suit, will we marry. If, instead, you do not want it, we'll find a way to cry off."

She stared at him, her mouth agape.

"You might find you like me after all. I come with a title and a lovely—if rather large—manor in Gloucestershire. Property well able to house a professional chemistry laboratory. There is also a large, well-staffed kitchen you could organize to suit yourself. It will house a large family too. Grandfather would—"

"Your grandfather would want better for you."

"Now you speak nonsense. While I'm perfectly happy to listen to your forceful opinions on many things, don't presume to tell me what my grandfather—or I—want."

"You're seriously considering this. Just because we were found locked in together last night?"

"That does add some urgency, but Bel, I planned to take my time to get to know you, to court you in the spring, and to show you to the Ton as the lovely treasure you are before I offered for you." His hand trembled as he touched her cheek. "You must admit we did take some advantage of our proximity last night."

She blushed a delightful pink. "I would like to get better acquainted," she admitted.

"Good. Because your aunt has insisted that we be formally betrothed. 'At the very least,' she said. They are sending the announcements to the papers. They're probably writing them up as we speak. They plan to announce it to the company tonight."

She gasped and raised both hands to cup her heated cheeks. She tipped her head back and stared at the ceiling for a moment before gazing back at him. "Aunt Flora will be torn between elation and jealousy that Aunt Violet got a jump on her."

That made them both laugh, the shared humor

warming his heart. "I should probably leave post haste to warn grandfather before it is in the papers," he said.

"Take me with you."

He wasn't sure he heard her. "What did you say?"

"Take me with you. I want to meet your grandfather and see this place where you think we might set up a full-scale chemistry laboratory. I might like a peek at the kitchen too."

John knew he must be grinning like a fool. He had her; he knew he had her. He leaned in for a kiss to set a seal on it. Soon enough they leaned back on the settee with Bel draped across his chest, and the kissing deepened. Her gentle fingers ran through his hair, sending tremors through them both.

"I take it I'm to wish you happy."

John saw Sophie over Bel's shoulder, and eased Bel back to the seat.

"Aunt Violet sent me to tell you you've been alone long enough. I could linger outside if you like," she grinned.

He was tempted, but he knew they would have other opportunities. They were, after all, betrothed. "Tell me Sophie, would you like to accompany your cousin to Gloucestershire to visit Wynnwood Hall?"

It must have been the right thing to say because the cousins were soon hugging and chattering in anticipation.

Chapter 13

TWO MONTHS later

Wynnwood Hall provided an impressive wedding breakfast, and Bel's aunts wondered how many succession houses had been emptied of flowers to fill it. The ladies lingered with their backs to a window that would have provided a panorama of the countryside while they sipped champagne and surveyed the room.

Between them, they counted three earls, two viscounts and a baron. Ridgemont's military colleagues had come to support him. The Duchess of Haverford herself attended as did her son the marquis. Bel's friend Merrilyn and her husband Sir Darius Finchwater, prominent in London's scientific set, chatted with the Earl of Westhampton, whose son Peter Hartley was also present. Cecil, of course, was nowhere to be found.

Their primary attention, however, was not on the guests.

"For someone who complained long and loud about not wanting to rush her, Ridgewood certainly made short work of it," Violet, Countess of Hartwell sniffed, studying the happy couple.

Flora, Marchioness of Gilford elbowed her sister. "Bel is positively radiant, as well she should be. She snatched a ducal heir, the catch of the year, right out from under the noses of the current crop of debutants."

"Not to mention, it is a love match," Violet sighed.

The two women stared at their niece, chatting with the Duke of Wynnwood and the Duchess of Haverford across the drawing room. She and her beloved had hovered in each other's orbit since the ceremony that morning in the village church, his hand finding hers often, hers touching him just as frequently.

"The duke certainly seems pleased. I'm delighted he has such a discerning eye for worth," Flora said.

The Duke of Wynnwood had taken Bel to his heart as soon as he met her.

"He must be. I understand he has commissioned a chemistry laboratory to be built on the grounds. Who would have thought he'd encourage Bel's peculiar interests," Violet added.

Laughter from the corner distracted her. Peter Hartley stood behind Sophie's chair, and two other young men were in attendance. "Now, Flora, what shall we do with Sophie? This association can't help but enhance her chances."

Flora studied her daughter smiling up at something Peter Hartley said to her. "My dear, Sophie can handle herself."

And so she could.

The End

Author's Note

I hope you enjoyed my little tale of vengeance and true love.

You have probably guessed that Bel's *cephaelis ipecacuanha* is the plant used to create what we now call ipecac syrup, once a staple of medicine cabinets as an antidote to accidental poisoning.

If you don't know about Sir Humphry Davy, you might want to read about him. A brilliant scientist, he was also quite handsome. He became a bit of a rockstar and women did actually flock to his public lectures, certainly not all of them drawn by his looks and charisma. He was an advocate for women's education at a time when few men were, causing no end of gossip and innuendo. However, he was quite religious, and is believed to have been faithful to his wife to whom he dedicated one of his major works, citing his "admiration of [her] moral and intellectual qualities."

If you'd like to read about "the incident" at the Duchess of Haverford's Venetian breakfast and the fate of

Bel's friends, with whom she had formed the Nemesis Collective, be sure to read *The Blossoming of the Wallflower* by Jude Knight.

Acknowledgments

No book reaches publication without the help of many people. This year in particular the author is grateful for the encouragement of more of her fellow readers and writers than she can list here. Particular thanks go to those who read and made suggestions in the early stages of writing, Judy Johnsen, Alina K. Field, Rue Allyn and to the editor of this book, Jude Knight.

Thanks is also owed to Amanda Mariee for setting up and leading the the Revenge of the Wallflowers multi-author series.

About the Author

Award winning author Caroline Warfield has been many things: traveller, librarian, poet, raiser of children, bird watcher, Internet and Web services manager, conference speaker, indexer, tech writer, genealogist—even a nun. She reckons she is on at least her third act, happily working in an office surrounded by windows where she lets her characters lead her to adventures in England and the far-flung corners of the British Empire. She nudges them to explore the riskiest territory of all, the human heart.

You can read her Regency and Victorian stories about families and friends, proper dukes and rogues, some set in small villages and massive ducal mansions, some in the outer islands, and some in places as far away as China on www.carolinewarfield.com.

Visit her on social media.

www.ingramcontent.com/pod-product-compliance
Lightning Source LLC
Chambersburg PA
CBHW022043170626
46808CB00003B/1339

Contents

Chapter 1

BELINDA WESTCOTT GAZED out the window of her uncle's fine carriage as it lumbered relentlessly over the frozen ruts of a narrow Northumberland road.

She wrapped her shawl tighter against the cold, certain she would rather ride outside in the frigid weather than listen to her cousin's incessant chatter. Sophie could be a dear, but not when she harped on Belinda's marriage prospects, sounding like her mother, Belinda's aunt, who had been unable to accompany them.

"Mama says you could have plenty of offers with the smallest of efforts this week."

Sophie's mother and Belinda's aunt, the Marchioness of Gilford, had lectured Belinda on the same subject endlessly after the latest Season passed with no offers of marriage. At least, none that got to her aunt and uncle. Belinda had become adept at deflecting unwanted attention in the six years since she had been "out." Her great humiliation of the year before, however, had kept most suitors away this past year.

"Mama says even at your age you could attract a

decent husband. Not a title, perhaps, but a decent man." Sophie hardly paused to draw breath.

Belinda gritted her teeth against the onslaught. *My age indeed. How much longer until we arrive at Hartwell Hall?* She didn't need or want some "decent man" offering for her out of pity.

"Mama says your dowry alone is enough to draw them."

Dowry! The very word stung. Belinda longed to use that money, a bequest from her grandmother, as she wished. She could purchase a small house and build a laboratory onto it so she could continue her chemistry studies in peace, but all three of her aunts, her mother's sisters, refused to consider such an outrage. Her uncles, who had control of the money since the death of Belinda's parents, merely laughed.

"Mama says there will be several eligible men at this house party."

Belinda rolled her eyes. "Cousin Cecil and some of his ramshackle friends?" she groaned. She loathed Cecil, who delighted in harassing her. More than one family member felt grateful he wasn't the heir. His older brother David served with Wellington in Spain. She prayed for him often. If he was killed, they would be stuck with Cecil.

Sophie shot her a pointed frown. "There will be others. I'm to drop hints about the dowry and encourage them to pursue you."

Belinda shuddered at the thought of Aunt Violet's son Cecil. He and his horrid friends made her life a misery whenever she encountered them in London. As to the others… The last thing she wanted was another set of fribbles pursuing her dowry, viewing her "odd starts" and bluestocking ways as merely the price they would have to pay for all that delicious cash.

Sophie drew breath and gazed at Belinda, guilt in her pale blue eyes. "Will that be a great bother, Bel? Hinting to them, I mean. I won't if you don't want it. You mustn't let the… difficulty—two years ago, I mean—bother you."

Belinda smiled at her cousin. She had a kind heart, and Belinda was fond of her when she wasn't parroting Aunt Flora. At seventeen and fresh from her first, very successful, Season, Sophie couldn't imagine any greater accomplishment than capturing a titled husband.

"You will be too busy to bother about me, Sophie. You're going to have a wonderful time," Belinda said.

Sophie sighed. "But Bel, you should too. Mama says you must not let Aunt Violet use you as some sort of unpaid servant. You are to enjoy the party."

"I won't," Belinda murmured. Aunt Flora wasn't to know that Belinda found Aunt Violet's house the most comfortable of the aunts' great manors. Violet, Countess Hartwell, believed that her house and particularly her kitchen ran better with Belinda in residence. "The meals are so much better when you direct the cook," she would say. It didn't occur to Aunt Violet that Belinda *was* the cook when she was in residence.

"Seriously, Bel. You almost disappeared last year when we visited. I hardly saw you the entire time," Sophie lamented. "I refuse to let Aunt Violet use you so."

"I promise we'll see each other, Sophie. Our rooms will be next to one another. Besides, I'll be staying on at Hartwell Hall after the party. I can assist Aunt Violet then."

Sophie sank back, mollified and quiet for once.

Belinda's mother's sisters had all married well, unlike Belinda's mother who happily wed the love of her life, a scholarly country squire, Lord Francis Westcott, third son of a marquess. Since her parents died eight years before, when she was fifteen, the aunts had passed her from hand to hand—not unkindly, but occasionally thoughtlessly. The kitchen at Hartwell Hall had become her favorite place. Mrs. Wesley, the cook, was happy to cede the work, and Belinda was free to explore the magic that was the chemistry of cooking. Uncle Hartwell had a fine scientific library, and she had even set up a small laboratory in an unused buttery off the kitchen. She quite looked forward to it.

Moments later Sophie bounced in her seat. "Mama says The Earl of Ridgemont will be in attendance," she trilled. "He is most certainly in search of a wife."

Belinda blinked, drawn out of her abstraction by Sophie's burst of enthusiasm. *Who?* Belinda wondered.

"Why is he coming?" She asked

"Because he is the Duke of Wynnwood's new heir, of course. The sudden death of cousin or something. Anyway, why else would he come to a house party?"

"Why indeed," Belinda murmured. The duke was an old man. She had no idea he had acquired a different heir. The previous one had been a profligate roué with wandering hands who slipped, unwed, into dissolute middle age. Belinda suspected Sophie was due for disappointment when she met the newly raised earl. He would be of similar age and no doubt the same proclivities.

Sophie didn't recognize Belinda's sarcasm. "Exactly. Wealthy and titled. He will need a wife. Getting him was quite a coup for Aunt Violet."

And a coup for the young lady who snags him, Belinda thought. The entire idea disgusted her.

The carriage lurched around a corner before Sophie could go on, and they drove up a lane flanked by the snow-covered skeletons of elm trees, bare now in early December. Sophie twisted in her seat, almost leaning out the window in excitement. "We're almost there! I can't wait."

Belinda's joy at arriving matched Sophie's, but it sprang from an entirely different source.

The door, opened by a footman, let in a blast of frigid air. Bel stepped down and shivered. The weather had been unusually freezing for days, especially here in Northumberland. A light snow covered the ground and more threatened.

The carriage bringing Susan, their shared maid, and footmen on loan from Aunt Flora for the house party, as well as their luggage, pulled up behind the cousins. The swift and attentive reaction to their arrival, a bowing butler and swarming servants, showed Aunt Violet's household stood on full alert. Guests must have been arriving in number that afternoon.

"Good day, Carlton!" The butler responded to Belinda's greeting with a proper bow and murmured "Welcome, Miss Westcott, Lady Sophie," while discreetly directing the disposal of baggage, horses, servants and carriages.

Aunt Violet fluttered about the entrance hall complimenting arriving debutantes, sympathizing with weary mamas, and preening over the apparent success of her party, if attendance could be the sole criteria.

Sophie spied friends from London and scurried off to join a giggling gaggle of girls. Belinda slid quietly toward the stairs.

"Belinda!" Aunt Violet's sharp call stopped her in her tracks. She sighed deeply, pasted a serene smile on her face and turned to greet her aunt.

The countess approached with a mixture of a dignified glide and unladylike urgency.

"Oh, my dear, thank goodness you're finally here. Flora kept you in London so long to spite me. I know she did,"

Aunt Violet said with a scowl and shuddering sigh. "Well, you're here now, and we'll make the most of it."

"How can I help, Aunt?"

Aunt Violet patted Belinda's hand where it lay on the banister. "I know you want to rest after that tedious journey, but I must trouble you to speak to Cook immediately. She won't listen to me; I don't know why I tolerate the woman, except she does so much better when you are here."

"Won't it keep for an hour or so?" Belinda asked plaintively. She really had hoped for a nap.

"You can rest after you speak to her. Last night's dinner was a disaster. Underdone potatoes, tasteless mutton, mushy fish," Aunt Violet hissed, attempting to whisper. "The earl frowned at his plate the entire meal. I wouldn't have asked him a day early if I knew you would be delayed." She glanced frantically around to see if she was overheard.

Ah yes. The eligible earl. Aunt Violet's "coup."

"I'll change my clothes and wash up. I can be down to the kitchen in a half hour," Belinda said, calculating how much time she needed to produce a decent dinner. She touched her aunt's arm. "Not to worry, Aunt Violet."

The countess didn't stop to thank her. She turned to greet more guests, and Belinda trudged up the stairs.

And so it begins, she sighed.

Chapter 2

"I SHOULD NEVER HAVE LET you spend so much time with my grandfather's valet!" John Conlyn, Earl of Ridgemont, scowled at the giant of a man who had once been his batman, with no more duties than to keep his uniform brushed and his gear packed for sudden moves. They had spent the previous year at John's grandfather's seat, Wynnwood Hall. Graves had become a fashion tyrant under the tutelage of the knowledgeable valet.

Graves frowned back. "Hold still. Ye need a decently tied cravat for dinner with those peers." He finished his efforts, stood back, and viewed his handiwork, nodding as he did. "Y'll do for a dinner. The ladies will approve."

The ladies. Graves never let an opportunity to remind him why they were here pass him by. *Grandfather's marching orders: find a decent girl of good family and marry her.* His emphasis was on decent, not bloodlines, thank the benevolent Providence. John smiled to himself.

The death of his cousin Frederick had pitched his grandfather into a year of mourning, and the old man dragged John with him. His grandfather had used every day of it to poke and prod John into what he said "will make you into a finer heir than Frederick ever was." Given the pox-ridden degenerate that was Frederick, John knew himself to be better the day the heirdom passed to him, but grandfather wasn't taking chances. He'd pulled John from the fleshpots of London to the family pile for a full twelve months of badgering—affectionate, but badgering all the same.

"Lift y'er chin, Jonny," Graves growled. "The old boy and that man of his pulled y'out of the muck you'd sunk into in Lunnan, and my job's to keep you up to snuff now we're on our own again."

Graves must be irritated if I'm Jonny again. John lifted his chin and Graves topped off his handiwork with a diamond pin, one of many gifts from his grandfather. "There. Now you look fine as can be, my lord." Graves gave a jerky nod.

A man might envy all those gifts if he didn't know every one of them came with strings tying John tighter and tighter to the Wynnwood estate. At least he had felt that way at first, while he mourned the loss of his military career, but, as the year went on, Grandfather's pride and the obvious needs of the tenants seeped into his soul. It would be a worthwhile life. Eventually. If only he could get used to it. Grandfather deserved his gratitude.

He sought his way down to the drawing room designated for pre-dinner gathering. He hesitated at the bottom of the stairs watching a group of young women—girls—tittering together as they entered the room, followed by two stately matrons, obviously the proud mothers of at least two of them.

Babies the lot of them. John couldn't imagine taking one to wife. *Courage, Conlyn!* He stood straighter, but stayed fixed in place.

As he paused, a footman rushed out the dining room

door, leaving it open. He watched the staff preparing for the guests and groaned.

The previous night's dinner had been so atrocious he regretted coming. *Surely it won't be as bad tonight.* At least he prayed so. He'd had his share of awful food in the Peninsula; he couldn't take a week of bad dinners.

He was about to move on when the woman directing the work caught his attention and his breath held. He couldn't say why. She was no diamond, and yet she was too well dressed to be cook or housekeeper. Too well even to be a governess or other upper servant. Still, she wasn't garbed as fashionably as the other guests either.

Oddly, he couldn't shake the feeling he knew her, although he couldn't place her. Taller than average, her lush curves, outlined in a simple gown, stirred him. The hair arranged high on her head was a rich chestnut, but what held his attention was the graceful slope of her neck. Most intriguing of all was her air of confidence and command. It made her far more interesting than the silly misses he'd seen so far. He shook his head. Ogling servants, even obviously superior ones, was not why he came.

John fixed on a haughty expression he'd learned from his grandfather, one he found useful as a shield, approached the drawing room, and joined the waiting guests. Countess Hartwell swanned up to him, glowing with smug delight. "Welcome to our humble gathering, my lord. May I introduce you to our new arrivals?"

She didn't wait for him to respond, but gripped his arm with iron determination. His heart sank at her destination, when she dragged him toward the group of young girls he'd seen earlier. Their faces and gowns ran together, none standing out from the other, as if England produced pattern card debutantes on demand.

That's unkind, John!

It was. He ignored the eager ones and focused on the shyest among them, smiling to set them at their ease.

"And this is my niece, Lady Sophie Gilray, daughter of the Marquess of Gilford," the countess crooned.

Ah. When he accepted, he had thought he might have an easier time at this house party as the guest of a house with no marriageable daughter. He should have expected a niece. He bowed over her hand and was struck by the twinkle of humor in Lady Sophie's open expression. He saw intelligence as well. This one might be worth his attentions. They chatted briefly when the countess fluttered off, having met her objective, to gossip with cronies.

Most of the simpering misses were as insipid in their conversation as he expected.

Lady Sophie grinned at him. "She's positively preening. Don't let her irritate you."

He followed her line of sight to where the countess stood nose high, making a spirited pronouncement to the other matrons. He hoped it wasn't an announcement of his engagement to her niece. Already.

Another lady joined his circle, managing to gracefully cut out most of the others. This one appeared just a bit older in years but far more worldly than the sweet things.

She pinned Lady Sophie with a brittle smile. "Dear Lady Sophie, could you introduce me to your new friend? Surely at an informal party protocol and all that fuss is unnecessary," she cooed.

Lady Sophie's expressive face wished the interloper to perdition so obviously that the other young woman must see it. She'd been left with little choice. "Miss Dinah Beckwith, may I introduce you to the Earl of Ridgemont. My lord, Miss Beckwith." Sophie's rigid jaw clipped her words.

"Earl? Oh my, I'm honored. I wonder if you know my grandfather, the Marquess of Delacourt? Perhaps you've